A CHANGED AGENT

ALSO BY TRACEY J. LYONS

The Women of Surprise Series

A CHANGED AGENT

TRACEY J. LYONS

Waterfall
PRESS

Text copyright © 2016 by Tracey J. Lyons

Published by Waterfall Press, Grand Haven, MI

www.brilliancepublishing.com

Amazon, the Amazon logo, and Waterfall Press are trademarks of Amazon.com, Inc., or its affiliates.

ISBN-13: 9781503934818
ISBN-10: 1503934810

Cover design by Kirk DouPonce, DogEared Design

Printed in the United States of America

This book is for my grandchildren, Nicholas, Colyn, Christopher, and Caroline—you are my inspiration. And for my husband, TJ, who has been there for me since the beginning.

Chapter One

"My trunk!" Elsie Mitchell watched in horror as her trunk fell off the over packed porter's wagon, spilling its contents onto the platform at the Albany train station. Grasping at her skirts, she ran along the damp cobblestones to rescue her garments. The porter rushed to right the trunk while Elsie knelt in the cold drizzle and began stuffing her skirts and blouses back inside. "Thank you for your help."

Steadying the trunk, he said, "I'm afraid I got caught up wanting to get everyone to the train on time and I overloaded the cart." The rotund man looked at her in dismay. "There won't be another train heading up to the Adirondacks until next week."

Elsie cast a furtive glance at an older well-dressed couple who scurried by her. A plume of black smoke belched from the great engine. She had to be home later today. After a two-week break, she needed time to prepare for the upcoming school session. She gathered up another blouse and a lace petticoat, cramming them inside the trunk. "I must be on this train." Needing the porter's help, she reached into her reticule, retrieving a coin from the last of her travel allotment. She gave the money to him.

An older woman stopped by and whispered some words to the porter, who shook his head. Then she opened her hand to show off not one but two coins. Giving Elsie a brief "Sorry, miss," he hurried off to earn the tip.

If she was to make this train, there wasn't a moment left to give the porter's desertion another thought. She knelt among her things, praying she'd be able to leave today.

The answer to her prayer came in the form of a Good Samaritan who bent down next to her, handing her a pair of white pantaloons. Ever so grateful for the extra help, Elsie took them and then gasped in shock when she realized the hand helping her belonged to a man ruggedly dressed like a lumberjack about to head up the mountain. A thick, reddish-brown beard covered most of his face, making it hard for her to discern what he really looked like.

"Thank you, but I don't need any help." Embarrassed that this stranger had a full view of her underthings, she avoided meeting his gaze, quickly putting the garment in the trunk.

"The train will be pulling out in a few minutes. I'm thinking you mean to get on board before then," he said.

Deciding it would be better to accept this benevolent stranger's help than miss the train, Elsie gave him a brisk nod. Past his shoulder she spotted two young children standing a short distance behind him, a boy and a girl, similar in height. Elsie guessed them to be about seven or eight years old. Safely under the cover of the platform canopy, the boy held the girl's hand snugly inside his while she had her free arm wrapped securely around a rag doll with golden hair that was a near match to the child's. Elsie straightened for a better look at them, her heart thudding against her rib cage.

As a schoolteacher in the Adirondack mountain village of Heartston, New York, where she was returning, Elsie prided herself on how intuitively she knew the needs of her students. And now captivated by the expressions on these little ones' faces, she couldn't take her eyes from the pair.

The children seemed to be watching them, their expressions lost and forlorn. She swung her gaze back to the man helping her, asking, "Are those children with you?"

"They are."

When a moment passed and he offered no more explanation, her natural curiosity had her wondering where he'd come from and where he would be heading with the children. They looked so alone. What had happened to them? There didn't seem to be anyone other than this man accompanying them. She wondered where their mother was. She said, "I can handle the repacking of my trunk. You should get back to your children."

"The children are fine, and I've no doubt you can finish this on your own." The stranger's mouth quirked upward, and then he said, "But if you don't get a move on, you're going to miss the train. So why don't you let me be of service?"

Much to her vexation, he began again to hand her odds and ends of undergarments. Shaking his head, he asked, "How can one woman possibly need all these things?"

She thought surely his wife must have all these basics in her wardrobe. Her heart skipped a beat when she saw him pick up a pair of black stockings. These were one of the few things she splurged on with her schoolteacher's salary, and she didn't want him to ruin them. She forced herself to stand stock-still as they slipped through his worn fingers into her outstretched hand.

Elsie put the stockings in the trunk, then pushed the lid down, only to be met with resistance. Leaning her full weight into it, she let out a very unladylike grunt. When that didn't work, she sat on top of the trunk, trying to push the bulging mess closed.

She gave one last little wiggle, hoping that would do the trick. She felt the gentleman's hand on her shoulder. She stood, stepping aside to give him room to try his luck. Laying his large hands on top of the stubborn trunk, he pressed down hard. The top resisted his strength, too.

"I think I see the problem." Settling the open lid back on its hinges, he reached in and pulled out a small pistol that had jammed itself in the hinge when the trunk was upended.

He dangled the butt of the gun between his forefinger and thumb.

"The derringer was a gift from my father." She'd pleaded with him for the chance to travel unchaperoned, and he had finally given in, agreeing to let her go unaccompanied only if she carried the pistol for protection.

She took the gun from the stranger's hand and confidently placed it in the only empty space left in the trunk.

"And this?" He held up the black leather-bound Bible with a questioning look.

"If you must know, my mother insists I travel with one of our family's Bibles."

Now he didn't hide his wide grin. "You sound like an interesting woman, one who travels with petticoats, a pistol, and the Good Book. Though it seems to me the book and the gun won't do you any good locked away in your trunk."

"There wasn't room in my travel bag for any of it."

Finally able to slam the trunk shut, she secured the lock and motioned for the porter to put it on the train. Turning, she quickly thanked the man who had helped her, hiked up her skirts, took one last look at the children, and boarded the train.

Shaking his head, William Benton watched the young woman disappear into the train car. Wrangling with the pretty young lady with the astonishing violet eyes had been the one bright spot in his week.

He glanced over at the two small children in his company—the little girl who hadn't spoken to anyone other than her brother since the day of their parents' death and the boy who protected her. Seven-year-old twins, Minnie and Harry Harper were the children of his late sister and brother-in-law, Amelia and Jason.

Mustering up a smile, Will made his way over to them. He'd been preparing for this trip from Albany to Heartston while recovering from a gunshot wound. The relocation had been planned. The hole in his shoulder and taking in the children had not. As a Pinkerton agent, William Benton's life was a secret. Even his family had no idea how he'd been making a living. They thought he was a drifter. Which was why he still couldn't believe his older sister, Mary Beth, had arrived on his doorstep earlier this week expecting him to take in these children with no more than a mere minute's notice.

Helping the children gather their belongings, he led them to the steps where they would board the train.

Looking down at the two little ones, Will felt a heaviness settle in his heart. He couldn't begin to imagine the changes these children had had to bear over the recent months. And now they were dependent on the likes of him.

Squatting down to be at eye level with them, he asked, "Have you two been on a train before?"

"Nope. I read about them in a book Ma bought me for Christmas last year," Harry replied. Scuffing his toe in the dirt, the boy looked downright dejected. "Aunt Mary Beth threw it away. She said it was too tattered to keep."

Swallowing hard, Will forced down the anger he was feeling toward his sister. "Looks like we'll just have to find you a better book."

"Okay," the boy replied, even though he didn't sound very convinced. "Uncle Will, how long is this train ride going to take?"

"We'll be there before sundown."

A fleeting look crossed the boy's face as he gave his sister's hand a quick squeeze. Will didn't have time to discern what all that could mean because it was their turn to board. As he escorted the children onto the train, he couldn't help what came naturally to him. He cautiously scanned the space around them to find some empty seats.

Seated to their right was an older couple. Up ahead was a young man slouched down with a cowboy hat pulled low over his brow, and in the row behind him sat the young woman with eyes the color of spring violets. Will noticed she'd gotten herself in order and her black hair was now tucked up under her plain brown bonnet.

He couldn't resist tipping his hat to her when they walked by. He barely made eye contact with her before she turned her head to stare out the soot-stained window. He gave a slight shake of his head, amused by how set she was on ignoring him. He settled the children in some empty seats five rows past her. Minnie and Harry shared the inside seat while Will took the aisle one. Stretching out his long legs, he crossed his feet at the ankles, staring ahead at the seat back in front of him.

He liked to use his travel time to think about his next assignment. According to the updated dossier he'd received last week, there was intelligence reporting that the thief the agency had been tracking could be making his way to the mountains with stolen railroad bonds worth thousands of dollars.

Masquerading as a foreman for the Oliver Lumber Company, Will had let his hair and beard grow long as part of his disguise. He swept his hand down the length of his scraggly beard in frustration. How was he going to be able to do his assignment and care for these children at the same time? Would he be able to provide a decent home for them once they arrived in Heartston? At least he'd had the wherewithal to send a telegraph to his Pinkerton contact in Heartston two days ago informing him of his change in circumstance. The reply had been simple . . . his charges would be looked after.

Not knowing what to expect, Will was certain of one thing: his priorities had changed. He'd gone from a loner to a man who had two children trusting him with their lives. He would not leave these children in the care of just anyone. Trust and faith had never come easy for him, and now both were being tested. The sharp twinge of pain in his arm reminded him that things could go wrong in an instant. Getting shot hadn't been in his plan when attempting to capture the pickpocket, but he was dedicated to his job and what it stood for. He knew full well that once a Pinkerton's real identity was discovered, he was rendered useless.

They were two hours into the train ride when it became apparent to Will that something was drastically wrong with Minnie. Her face had become as white as a sheet, and the poor girl was clutching her brother's hand so tightly her knuckles were bleached. The hairs on the back of Will's neck prickled as a sense of unease settled over him like a dark storm cloud. Leaning forward in his seat, Will whispered to Harry, who looked as scared as he felt. "Harry. What's wrong with your sister? She doesn't look well."

The boy's lower lip trembled. Turning toward him, the boy whispered, "I think it's her stomach. She gets sick whenever we travel."

Suddenly Will remembered the look the two of them had exchanged before boarding the train. He had a feeling that sooner rather than later Minnie would be emptying her stomach.

He spotted one of the wrappers that had held the sandwiches they'd eaten when they first boarded the train. Minnie made a strange sound. Just as her mouth opened, Will shoved the wrapper underneath her quivering chin. *Who knew that small of a stomach could hold so much food?* Will thought grimly as he opened the window and tossed the offending wrapper out. Pulling a handkerchief from his pocket, he did his best to wipe her face and hands.

The poor girl was shivering. He didn't know what to do. He reached out to her, but Minnie shrank back toward her brother. He felt all thumbs and realized with a tug in his chest that his efforts were woefully inadequate. If he couldn't handle an upset stomach, what was he going to do when something major happened?

From her seat Elsie heard the retching sounds. Peering around, she saw the gentleman who'd helped her earlier trying to comfort the little girl. Her heart went out to the child, for she knew firsthand how terrible motion sickness could be. Reaching into her reticule, she saw the large envelope her former fiancé had entrusted to her care a few days ago. He'd asked the favor of her taking it to Heartston for safekeeping until he could come for it. She paused, remembering their awkward meeting in Albany, then pushed it aside. Groping around the bottom of the bag, she found the peppermint stick lodged at the bottom.

Brushing the nasty coal cinders—which seemed to seep in from every nook and cranny in the train car—from her skirt, she rose. The motion from the train jostled her to and fro, threatening to send her spilling onto the floor. Grabbing hold of the seat back in front of her, she steadied herself. And then Elsie gingerly made her way down the narrow aisle to the family.

Stopping at their seats, she said in a gentle voice, "She is suffering from motion sickness. I've some peppermint she can suck on. That should help soothe her queasiness."

The man turned halfway around in his seat to look at her. The flat brim of his well-worn black hat tipped back on his brow, which gave Elsie a full view of his dark eyes. She caught the flash of recognition when he saw her. Thin lines surrounded the corners of his eyes. Now that she had time to take a closer look at him, she could see the clothes he wore looked clean. Yet his duster coat had wear marks at the elbows and his trousers were thin at the knees. In sharp contrast, the children were dressed in what looked to be brand-new coats. There was nary a wrinkle on them, the fabric crisp and clean.

The children looked so tired. The poor little girl's face had turned a chalky white. Her shoulders hunched together as shivers overtook her. The little boy patted her on the shoulder.

"I'll give her the peppermint." The man spoke calmly as his brooding gaze briefly met hers.

The same unnerving feeling Elsie had had when she'd taken her stockings from him on the train platform settled over her. It was as if in that one quick glance, he'd taken in every detail of her face right down to the smallest freckle. He held his hand open, and she placed the peppermint stick in his palm. His fingers tightened around hers.

A frisson of awareness snaked its way along her spine. Elsie didn't want to think about her physical reaction to this stranger. She'd given her heart to Virgil Jensen, and he'd abandoned her without any regard for her feelings. Ever since then she'd devoted her life to the young children who crossed the threshold into her classroom. The work left her without any time to fall in love again.

"Thank you" was all he said.

Elsie swallowed, forcing out a response: "You're welcome."

As he turned his attention back to the children, she offered up one more bit of advice before heading back to the safety of her seat. "She should be sitting on your lap. It will help to improve her stamina if she can see out the window."

"Might I know your name now?" he inquired.

"Elsie Mitchell."

Tipping his hat to her, he said, "I'm William Benton."

"A pleasure to meet you, Mr. Benton."

"You, too, Miss Mitchell."

Then, in a rustling of skirts, she rushed back to her seat.

The weather began to change on the trip north. As the engine chugged along the Hudson River, the steady rain became a light but persistent drizzle. When at long last the train pulled into the Heartston station, Will helped the children off. They were met by the sight of fat spring snowflakes and a tall beanpole of a man.

"Mr. Benton? I'm Roy Wells. John Oliver sent me to fetch you and the youngsters."

Will shook the man's hand, then gathered the children to wait for their trunks to be unloaded. Out of the corner of his eye he watched for Miss Mitchell, wondering if this would also be her stop. Then he saw her step down from the car onto the platform. Wells approached her, too, tapping her on the shoulder to get her attention. Pulling his hat low, Will observed them, listening in on their exchange with interest.

"Miss Mitchell, we were hoping you'd be on this train!"

"Good afternoon, Mr. Wells. And who might this *we* be that you're talking about?"

"Mr. Oliver. He needs to see you straight away."

Will knew he was expected to report in to Agent Oliver, but why did he need to see Miss Mitchell?

"Can't he wait until I've had time to settle in?"

With a fervent shake of his head, Wells replied, "No, miss. He said you are to come as soon as you've arrived."

"I have to wait for my trunk."

"I'll fetch yours and Mr. Benton's and bring them over to Mr. Oliver's office. You have to go now."

Will looked up to find Miss Mitchell standing with her hands gripping her reticule, watching him with those clear violet eyes. He knew she had the same questions he did: What was so urgent that John Oliver required both of them? What did they have in common other than being on the same train? And the most troublesome question for him was, would she somehow become a part of his mission? He hoped not. Will preferred to work alone. He began to formulate a plan in the event Agent Oliver suggested Miss Mitchell become part of his assignment.

"I guess we'd best get moving," he said, keeping his thoughts to himself. With a gentle nudge of his hand, Will urged the children forward, following Miss Mitchell down the planked walkway.

The train station was at one end of town, which had been settled in the midst of thick pine forests and craggy mountains. Drenched in thick gray clouds, the distant high peaks of the Adirondack Mountains were barely visible. The pungent scent of freshly milled lumber mingled with the acrid coal smell coming from the train and made his nose itch. Trying to keep pace with the young woman who was charging down the main street as though a pack of wolves were nipping at her heels, Will hurried the children along.

Abruptly turning to the right, they continued down a narrow alleyway where a black sign with an arrow and gold lettering hung off to one side of a two-story building, pointing the way to the lumber company's office. They stopped in front of a door bearing the markings of the Oliver Lumber Company. Feeling the tingle of unease creep between his shoulder blades, Will sensed whatever was about to happen hadn't been a part of the original arrangement. But then again, nothing in the past few days had gone accordingly, so why should this meeting be any different?

Squaring his shoulders, Will let the children and the young lady go ahead of him into a dimly lit room, an annex housing a small desk, some barrels with "Nails" stenciled in black on the lid, a stack of crates, and a rough-hewn counter area. No one was there, so he moved toward a closed door on the opposite side of the room. He knocked once.

"The door's open." A man's rich baritone voice sounded from behind the door.

Removing his hat, Will ushered the children and Miss Mitchell into a smaller room that served as the office. The space was sparsely furnished. Pausing in front of the oak desk, he said, "I'm William Benton."

"John Oliver." Rising from his chair, Will's superior came around to the front of the desk with his hand outstretched. They shook hands.

"It's a pleasure to finally meet my newest employee. And I see you and Miss Mitchell have already met."

Will glanced at the young woman who stood with her hands folded in front of her. He saw movement beneath her skirt and realized she'd begun tapping her toe.

Taking a wide-legged stance, John Oliver folded his arms across his massive chest, looking from one of them to the other, sizing them up. Will thought himself to be tall at just under six feet, but this man had to be at least two inches over that in height. Because Agent Oliver's dark hair was graying at the temples and wrinkles fanned out around his sharp blue eyes, Will guessed him to be about thirty-five years old. He'd heard of John Oliver's adventures as a Pinkerton agent and knew the man could be a force to be reckoned with.

A feeling of unease worked its way along his spine.

"How was your trip?" Oliver asked.

"My trip went well, sir."

"I'm glad to hear it." Now he looked at the young woman. "I don't know if you're aware, Mr. Benton, but Miss Mitchell is Heartston's schoolteacher. And a mighty fine one she is. I take it your trip to Albany was restful, Miss Mitchell?"

"I had a lovely visit with my aunt and uncle. But, Mr. Oliver, why did you need to see me in such a hurry? I would have liked time to freshen up from my trip first." She managed to put a smile on her face. And though her smile seemed sincere enough, Will noticed her toe kept right on tapping.

"I beg your forgiveness for my ill manners, but I've a proposition for you involving Mr. Benton and his charges."

The foot hidden beneath the skirts stilled. "I can't imagine, other than the schooling of the children, what Mr. Benton and I would have to do with one another."

"Hmm. That makes two of us," Will mumbled, even though he knew full well where this conversation seemed to be heading as he watched Oliver grin from ear to ear.

"You see, Miss Mitchell," Oliver said, "I've come up with a solution that will solve both of your problems!"

"I don't have any problems," she quickly countered.

"But you do. Mr. Benton needs someone to help him care for his niece and nephew while he begins his new job at my lumber company, and you"—he paused to point a finger at her—"you have made no secret of the fact that you suffer from a bit of wanderlust. Why, just the other day our friend Miss Amy Montgomery mentioned how you were going to be helping her out at the bakery so you could plan your next trip. This, in addition to the extra tutoring you've taken on. You've been scrimping and saving for months. I can't imagine how you have any spare time at all, Miss Mitchell."

He leaned closer to her, setting the snare. "I know how you yearn to expand your traveling horizons for the benefit of your students, and I've found a way for you to do just that."

Will could all but see the wheels turning in her head as she put two and two together and came up with the four of them. Her delicate jaw, which only seconds ago had been clenched, dropped open.

And then she just as quickly snapped it shut and said, "You want me to help him care for his niece and nephew? I can't imagine adding another job to my already full plate."

"If you decide to help Mr. Benton with the children, it will enable you to drop one of those jobs. I've taken all of your needs into consideration. My grandmother's house has been vacant for almost a year. Will and the children can live in the main portion of the house. There's a small apartment attached that would be suitable for you to occupy.

Really all you need to do is make sure the children have someone to watch over them when their uncle is working."

"You have assumed an awful lot here, Mr. Oliver. I'm just not sure about taking on this extra responsibility."

"The job comes with a decent salary, Miss Mitchell."

Will could tell from the way she nibbled at her lower lip that she was thinking about taking the offer.

"I have been dreaming of a trip abroad," she said.

"Imagine how much your students would love to hear about those travels!" Pouring on the charm, he ended with, "Taking on this job can help you get what you wish for."

Her gaze settled on the children's upturned faces. Will watched as her expression softened in sympathy. Then she turned to him. The look she gave him was clearly more cautious.

"You say there is an apartment attached to your grandmother's house?" she asked Oliver.

Oliver nodded.

"I'll just need to be there to help when Mr. Benton is unable to?"

Again he nodded. "So you'll take the job?"

Chapter Two

Elsie knew little about William Benton, but as she looked at his niece's and nephew's faces, she was certain these children needed someone other than just their uncle to care for them. They needed a woman's touch. Mr. Oliver was correct. Having her help them would solve Mr. Benton's problem and enable her to save money for traveling. She could see the urgency in Mr. Benton's situation. Most importantly, Elsie felt in her heart that God was calling on her to do this.

Elsie answered Mr. Oliver's question with a yes. And then realizing she hadn't been introduced to the boy and girl, asked them, "And what might your names be?"

"The boy's name is Harry, and this is his twin sister, Minnie." Their uncle gently urged them forward. Minnie slid closer to her brother.

Elsie saw that they had similar oval-shaped eyes with the same blue-green hues. Minnie had a riotous head of curly blonde hair that begged to be tamed into a braid, while Harry's, though the same shade, was a bit straighter and in need of a good trimming. Minnie stood half a head shorter than her brother. Elsie was struck again by his protective nature.

Using a soft tone, she said, "You've come to town at just the right time. We're getting ready to start our next school session."

Their uncle asked, "How soon would I have to enroll the children, Miss Mitchell?"

"Classes begin bright and early tomorrow morning."

She saw Minnie take hold of her brother's hand and whisper in his ear.

Harry in turn tugged at his uncle's coat, craning his head to look up at him. "Uncle Will, Minnie doesn't want to go to another new school."

Elsie caught a flash of alarm in the man's eyes. Bending down to Minnie's level, she said, "You'll love our school, Minnie. We have a lot of fun, and you'll make new friends. I promise you'll be happy there."

Minnie hid her head behind her brother's back.

"Ah, I see. You're a shy one. Well, that's okay. I was shy once, too." Straightening, she looked at John Oliver. "I'll have to make the arrangements for my move, so it will be a few days before I can be with the children. Will that be all right?"

He looked at his new employee for affirmation and then gave her a quick nod.

"Then I'll be heading home." Rearranging the bonnet on top of her head, Elsie prepared to step back out into the inclement weather. Pausing, she looked at Mr. Benton.

"About the school, Mr. Benton. Don't wait too long to get them signed up. It's best if they start with the rest of the class. That way it will be easier for them to form friendships and not be coming in when the others are all settled."

Gathering the twins closer, he assured her, "We'll be by tomorrow."

The door closed behind Miss Mitchell with a hollow sound. Will settled the twins on a bench in front of the window, safely out of the way, so he could continue his conversation without the children overhearing. His boss spoke in a hushed voice. "How's the shoulder wound?"

"I'm on the mend. Care to explain why you made these arrangements without consulting with me first?"

Agent Oliver stroked his clean-shaven chin. "I understand about family, Will, but I'm not sure how you thought you were going to provide for them *and* do your job. Having the schoolteacher help you out is the only thing to do."

Moving to the far side of his desk, the man leaned against it and continued, "Now you've brought them here promising them what, exactly? Not to mention you may be bringing them into a situation that could prove dangerous. Miss Mitchell agreed to do the job, and she'll do right by you and the children."

"I agree with what you've said, Agent Oliver. But there has to be a better way to make this work for everyone."

It was clear to Will that the young schoolmarm had not taken to him. Her wariness of him could present problems down the road if she couldn't put her trust in him. Will needed her to believe he was the new foreman for the Oliver Lumber Company. On the brighter side, he could tell by the way her gaze softened when she looked at Harry and Minnie that she would be kind to them. He figured that had to count for something.

"Right now," his boss said, "all you have are some trunks and a promise of one room for you to sleep in tonight. I can tell from the set of your jaw that handing them off to another family for safekeeping isn't going to be an option."

Drawing himself up to his full height, Will replied, "No, sir, it is not."

Leaving his perch on the desk, his superior walked around to the back of it. "My grandmother's house is two streets over. It will need to be cleaned up and there are some sparse furnishings, enough to keep you and the children comfortable. Miss Mitchell can furnish her apartment as she sees fit."

"Yes, sir."

Will worried that once she'd had some time to think about what she would be getting into, she might have a change of heart. He needed another plan in case this one didn't work out. "Is there anyone else in town who can help out in case the schoolteacher backs out?"

Raising an eyebrow, Oliver replied, "Have you seen the size of this town, Will? There aren't all that many females of an age who can tend to your children. I assure you that the teacher will do a just service for you."

"I need to be clear about one thing. I am not going to use the children as part of my cover."

"The children by default will be a part of this, Agent Benton. I trust you will keep them safe."

John Oliver's comment didn't leave any room for argument.

"What about Miss Mitchell? Once she moves into the apartment, how will I keep her from finding out who I really am? I don't need to put anyone else in danger."

"I suspect you'll find a way."

Pulling out his chair, Oliver sat down, shuffled through a stack of papers, and said, "I imagine the children must be tired and a bit hungry. You can use the one room we spoke about earlier for tonight, since it's clean and the bed's made up. Settle in, and then the three of you can come to my house for supper. Tomorrow will be soon enough for you to see about the other quarters for your family and Miss Mitchell."

Though he was thankful to Agent Oliver for offering up the spare room at the back of his office, the one thing Will hated was to have a cold nose, and when he awoke to bright sunlight flooding through the only window in the narrow room, his nose was cold. Rubbing his sleeve across it, he slowly opened his eyes to find two matching sets of blue-green eyes staring down at him.

"Good morning, Uncle Will." Harry's breath was a thin vapor in the chilly morning air. "We're hungry . . . and cold." His teeth chattered.

In her arms Minnie held tightly to Hazel the doll.

Will pushed aside the blankets he'd made a bed out of on the floor last night. He walked over to the small stove and added some wood to the fire he'd banked.

The children sat on the edge of the single bed, watching him.

"I've got to go use the necessary," he grumbled, not used to having an audience.

Minnie giggled and Harry said, "We already went."

That meant they'd been outside without him knowing they'd left the room. He must have been more tired than he'd thought. Pausing with one hand on the doorknob, he glanced over his shoulder and warned, "I don't like you wandering around without telling me where you're going."

"We didn't want to wake you up." Harry shrugged, adding, "I remembered where it was from last night when you took us."

Angry with himself for sleeping through their movements, Will said, "From now on you tell me when you're leaving."

"Sure, Uncle Will. When you get back can we eat?"

Nodding, Will left them to attend to his business.

He returned a few minutes later to open the basket containing blueberry muffins that Oliver's housekeeper had sent them off with last night. Handing one to each child, he took the last one for himself, longing for a cup of strong black coffee to accompany it. Biting into the muffin, he worried how they were going to react when he told them they would be going off to school today.

There was no sense putting off the inevitable. "Harry and Minnie, I'm going to be taking you to school today."

"Why can't we stay with you?" Harry asked.

Minnie stopped chewing to look up at him. Her round eyes widened, and he could see the tears starting to well. There was no other choice. They couldn't stay with him.

"I can take care of Minnie while you work, Uncle Will."

He knelt in front of them. Will suspected that over the past months Harry had stepped up to take care of his sister many times. But he didn't need to do so now.

"You can't be here alone. Besides," Will tried to reassure them, "Miss Mitchell is looking forward to seeing both of you today." He didn't know whether this was true, considering he hadn't decided to do this until this morning. It seemed the children had taken a liking to the schoolteacher. So a little bit of coaxing couldn't hurt.

Throwing his half-eaten muffin on the floor, Harry choked back a sob. Then he tried to push past Will, who grabbed the lad before his feet could hit the floorboards, setting him back on the bed. Harry sat with his arms folded tightly across his chest, scrunching his eyes together.

Will saw a small tear form at the corner of one of Harry's eyes. He didn't know what to do to make the situation better for them. He wasn't a parent. He was a spy. He could track and catch the worst criminal, but he had no idea how to handle heartbroken children.

Softly, he said, "Listen, I know this has been hard for you. But right now I'm all the two of you have. And today I have to take you to school because I need to get our new house together."

He stood up. "So do you think you and your sister can wash up so we can head on out?"

Scrubbing his hands over his face, Harry nodded.

Will walked down the main street with a child flanking each side and Hazel safely nestled in Minnie's little arms. The town meandered along a crooked roadway, with stores, a saloon, and a hotel lining one side. Across the street Will spotted the white clapboard church. Next to that was a fenced-in cemetery. Beyond that sat a single-story structure made out of log beams. A bell hung next to a set of white double doors.

He entered the single-room schoolhouse, savoring the warmth of the room. The first thing that caught his eye was the nicely rounded backside of Miss Mitchell as she bent over to pick up a book from the floor.

"Ooh!" She huffed out in surprise when she realized he was standing there.

Taking off his hat, he drawled, "Good morning, Miss Mitchell."

"It isn't polite to stare, Mr. Benton."

"I wasn't staring, Miss Mitchell. I was admiring the view." He grinned as a rosy blush brushed her cheeks. "At your suggestion, I decided to enroll the children in school."

Setting the book on the desk, she said, "I'm glad you brought them here. Why don't you children sit there at those two desks in the front row so I can get your information down?"

After the children were seated, she took out a leather-bound ledger and, flipping through the first few pages, found a clean sheet to write on.

"Minnie. Can you tell me your given name?"

Taking a step toward the children, Will rested a hand on the back of Minnie's chair. "Her name is Minnie Harper."

"It's best if she answers for herself, Mr. Benton. She needs to get used to interacting with me." Directing her gaze to Minnie, she asked, "Can you tell me how your reading is coming along?"

Minnie fidgeted in her chair, then stood up, walked over to Harry, and whispered in his ear. It was Harry who said, "She's halfway through the first-year primer, Miss Mitchell."

"You're doing quite well now, aren't you, Minnie?" Miss Mitchell looked over the top of the children's heads to Will. "Mr. Benton, might I have a word with you outside?"

He followed her out into the warming air. The sun was rising over one of the high peaks that surrounded the town, burning off the morning fog, drying the dewy grass, and warming the brisk spring air. Heartston was beginning to wake up. Will inhaled the smell of the fresh-baked bread coming from the bake shop. He watched as store owners hung out their "Open for Business" signs.

"The child's shyness is quite severe," Miss Mitchell said. "Do you know what the cause of it is?"

Turning the brim of his hat in his hands, Will pondered her question.

"Minnie and Harry's parents—my sister and her husband—died in an accident six months ago. As far as I know, she hasn't spoken to anyone other than her brother since then."

"I'm so sorry for your loss. This has to be a most difficult time for you and the children."

"Have you ever worked with a child with Minnie's ailment before?" Will asked.

"I haven't seen anything as acute as this. Has she been living with you since her parents' death?"

He shook his head. "I only took charge of them a few days ago." His remaining sister, Mary Beth, had taken custody of the children first. Then she'd selfishly decided to put her needs above theirs, telling Will there wasn't room in her life for children. She was a downright mean-spirited woman, set in her ways. He'd tried convincing her to keep Harry and Minnie until the fall, thinking that perhaps this particular assignment would be over and he'd be able to help out, but his words had fallen on deaf ears.

A myriad of emotions flickered through her violet eyes. "I see."

"What is that supposed to mean?" He hadn't meant to sound defensive, but he was tired and frustrated. He knew that Minnie's condition would get better with time; he just hoped it would be sooner rather than later.

Her hands went to her hips as she frowned at him. "It means that Minnie will have to be handled with special care. I imagine it's a very big thing for those children to be in a new place, with a new parent, and now having to make new friends. Don't you understand how that might feel, Mr. Benton?"

Narrowing her eyes, she studied him, and then, with her head cocked to one side, her gaze softened. "Or are you one of those so hardened by life that you can't even care?"

His hackles rose. "Look here, lady, I cared enough to bring them with me to this town while I'm starting a new job! I cared enough to agree to bring you into their new home. And I cared enough to bring them to school today."

"Raising children is more than just putting them in school for the day. But I suspect most single men in your position would have left them at the nearest orphanage. So I do commend you for taking them in."

Despite his anger, he managed to say thank you as he looked beyond her to the children streaming into the school yard. "It must be near time to start your day."

She waved to a few of the students as they began climbing the steps.

A little girl with dark-haired pigtails tugged at her skirt. "Miss Mitchell, I can write my *A*'s perfectly. I practiced on our break, just like you told me to."

"Good job, Clara." She patted the child on the back. "Why don't you go in and sit in the front row today? We have some new students, and I think you'll be just the one to help them out."

"Thank you, Miss Mitchell!" Beaming, the girl ran up the rest of the steps into the classroom.

Will didn't want to leave the children. The feeling was unexpected. He'd thought he'd be happy to leave them in good hands while he took the time he needed to get settled. Instead, his stomach twisted into a ball of knots. What if Minnie thought he was abandoning her?

"Let me come back inside to say good-bye to Harry and Minnie." He waited while she went ahead of him up the stairs. "Is there some paperwork I need to fill out?"

"No. I can have them tell me, or rather, Harry can tell me about their schooling. Simple testing should indicate where they left off in their studies."

The excited chatter of the students spilled out the door. Following the teacher into the room, he began to feel marginally better about leaving the twins in her care. But then he noticed the metal lunch buckets lined up below the coats in the open coat closet. It never occurred to him to make lunches for the children.

"I didn't pack lunches for Harry and Minnie."

"Please, don't worry, Mr. Benton. I always bring extra just in case." She smiled up at him. "The children will be fine, trust me. Children are some of God's most resilient creatures."

"Thank you."

"For what?"

"For putting my mind at ease."

"It's all part of my job. And you're welcome. Now come say your good-byes."

The students gathered around her as she walked up the wide aisle, each of them vying for her attention. It became even clearer to Will how much they adored her. He spotted Clara sitting on the right side of Minnie. Harry was dutifully keeping a watch on his sister. Will wished even harder for Minnie's speech to return so that the boy could make new friends on his own. Hearing his heavy-booted footfalls, they turned to look up at him.

Squatting next to Harry, he said, "I have to leave now. You'll be in good hands with Miss Mitchell. Don't give her any trouble."

"We'll be good, Uncle Will."

Minnie hugged Hazel closer to her chest, looking at him without a smile, and Will thought he saw a well of wariness and a few unshed tears in her eyes. Knowing he was leaving them in capable hands helped him exit the building alone.

His boss had given him the rest of the week to settle in, making it very clear there were two things he had to accomplish in that time. He had to get the house livable for the children and see that the apartment was put in order for Miss Mitchell.

Following the directions Oliver had given him, Will found the house on South Street. It was in better shape than he'd imagined. The white clapboard, two-story building stood on a corner lot. A picket fence surrounded the front yard. A few pickets were missing here and there. The front porch, though sagging, would suffice. He could see where the steps had been recently repaired.

Unlocking the front door, he entered a narrow, musty-smelling hallway through a curtain of cobwebs. Brushing the webs from his clothes, he moved farther into the house. The wide floorboards creaked under his feet. To the right was a small room that probably had served as a parlor at one time. On the left was a doorway that led to a large kitchen with a cook stove and a sink. Brushing aside more cobwebs, he made his way to the staircase. The newel post was shaky, and a few of the steps creaked under his weight. Upstairs there were three bedrooms. He thought it would be nice for each of them to have their own, but he worried that Minnie wouldn't want to be separated from her brother.

Back downstairs he found a doorway off the kitchen, leading to a small apartment. Here there was a bedroom, a small washroom, and a sitting area. He hoped Miss Mitchell could live in these sparse quarters. Remembering the silk stockings that had fallen out of her trunk at the train station, he knew she might expect more finery. It had been a long time since he'd shared a living space, and Will didn't know a thing about Miss Mitchell's habits.

Was she an early riser? From what he'd seen of the tidiness of the schoolroom, he guessed she would keep her rooms neat. And he never did ask if she knew how to cook. Good meals would be nice to come home to after a long day. Still, the one thing that set in his mind was the fact that he'd be sharing his life with another person, someone who might very well want to know about things he couldn't reveal.

As Agent Oliver had said, Will would have to figure out how to make this arrangement work. Backing out of the rooms, he felt satisfied he'd made the best decision. For him, this house seemed like a gift from God. With a solid roof over his head and sturdy floorboards beneath his feet, Will had no doubt he'd be comfortable settling in here. This house was a darned sight better than most places he'd laid his head. But for Miss Mitchell, it might not be enough. Still, the condition of the house would have to suffice. Will shouldn't be worrying over her . . . and yet he found the violet-eyed woman was never far from his thoughts.

If he was going to get through the chores, he couldn't ponder the situation any longer. He shut the door, going back into the cooking area to begin the inventory of the house's contents. By the time he was finished, he had a list of food supplies as well as another list detailing what repairs needed to be made. He didn't need to worry about the trunks because Roy Wells would have them brought over.

Going back through each room, he pulled the dusty white sheets off the furniture and opened a few windows to let out the musty smell. Never far from the back of his mind was the real reason he was here. On a normal assignment he would have already known where the contacts could be found, but then again this was as far from a normal assignment as one could get. But he was quite good at adjusting to the unexpected. After all, as a Pinkerton agent, he had to be. Finally feeling in control of the situation at hand, confident he could get the job done and provide for the children, he set about the rest of his day.

Leaving the house, he walked into the village. Unsure of where exactly the dry-goods store was located, he stopped a young lad who was busy sweeping the walkway in front of a shop to ask for directions.

He pointed down the street. "Heartston's Dry Goods is two doors on the right, past the telegraph office, mister."

Tipping his hat, Will followed the directions. The doorway outside the large two-story building was flanked by barrels and stacks of crates. A man stepped out from behind the ones to Will's right. He wore a long canvas apron and carried an armful of packages that were about to topple over.

"Howdy! Mind getting that door for me?"

"Sure thing." Will stepped in front of the man to get the door.

"Thanks. My wife is under the weather, so I'm working at our store by myself today."

Will followed him into the store, blinking at the items spread out before him. One side of the store held fabrics and sewing notions, while the other was filled with canned goods and every type of household utensil imaginable.

The man set the packages on the countertop. "What can I get for you?"

"I'm setting up a house. So I need cooking supplies. Canned food, sugar, flour. I'm sure there are a lot of things I'm forgetting."

Pushing his glasses up his nose, the man studied Will. "You new here in town?"

"I am."

"Thought so. I know everybody for miles in these parts. Sooner or later they all come here for supplies. I'm Francis Moore."

"Will Benton."

Francis stuck his hand out and Will shook it.

"Do you get a lot of new people here in Heartston?" Mr. Moore seemed like a fountain of information about the locals.

"Not so much. Usually just a few lumberjacks coming on for the season. Sometimes we get visitors off the weekly stagecoach. None that I noticed lately, though. Families like yours are few and far between." He took a pair of scissors from behind the counter and cut the string off one of the packages. Still holding the scissors, he asked, "If you don't mind my asking, where is this house of yours?"

"Over behind the church." Will saw that the package contained bolts of fabric.

"Only one place over there that's been empty. Ida Oliver's old place. Is that where you're staying?"

Will nodded.

"I'm surprised John is letting the place go."

"He's letting me live there as part of my salary with his lumber company."

Mr. Moore gave Will another once-over. "I guess you *could* be a lumberjack."

Will hid a grin, then walked over to the section of the store where the canned goods were kept.

"Give me your list, and I'll help you get started."

"I've got the list right here." He handed it to the man.

Mr. Moore glanced over the piece of paper and asked, "How many you buying for?"

"Three of us." Quickly, Will corrected himself. "No, make that four."

"You don't know how many you've got living in your house?" The man slanted him a look. "Kids?"

The man was sharp, no doubt about it. He'd make a good agent. "Two kids."

"Family of four, then." Joining him in the aisle, the man began handing Will all sorts of cans. When his arms were bulging and he feared he couldn't fit one more can inside them, the man added another can of beans and then ushered Will back to the counter.

The cans tumbled out of Will's grip onto the countertop.

"I expect you'll be needing a sack of flour, sugar, cornmeal . . . Didn't your wife bring any of that stuff with her when you moved here?"

"You sure are a nosy fella."

The man winked at him. "Just trying to make sure you got enough stores for your family."

"I think this will do." After paying for the goods and arranging to have the supplies delivered, Will left the store.

Then he made his way over to the schoolhouse to pick up Harry and Minnie. Brushing off his dusty pants and tucking in his shirttail, he realized he was even looking forward to seeing the schoolmarm again.

Chapter Three

All in all, Elsie thought Harry and Minnie's first day had gone well. The other children had been welcoming, and although Minnie hadn't left her brother's side, Harry managed to make a few new friends. Gently laying a hand on their shoulders, Elsie walked them out into the warm afternoon. She shielded her eyes from the bright sunlight and spotted Mr. Benton waiting at the bottom of the steps. He appeared to have had a hard day's work. His clothes still had a bit of dust and dirt smudges on them. Harry and Minnie scampered toward him.

"Uncle Will!" Harry practically threw himself into his uncle's arms, but at the last moment drew up short.

She noticed how their uncle held his arms at his sides, not reaching out when Harry came to him. He seemed to have no idea how to interact with the children. She longed to tell him that touching and holding Harry wouldn't bring either of them any harm.

Minnie followed at a slower pace. It broke Elsie's heart to know that the girl was in so much emotional pain and that Harry still wasn't sure about how to act around his uncle. She had no doubt that losing their parents had crushed their spirits.

"Hello, Harry," Mr. Benton said. "How was your first day at school?"

"It was good."

He looked up at Elsie for confirmation. She nodded. "They had a good first day, Mr. Benton. I take it you had a busy day without the children to distract you?"

"I was at the house, attempting to make it livable."

"That house hasn't been lived in for quite some time. There must have been a mess of spiderwebs to greet you."

"Spiderwebs and a mountain of dust." He tipped his hat back, revealing the dirt smudges on his forehead. For a brief moment Elsie wondered how he might look clean-shaven.

Then he said, "I plan to make it suitable for all of us in no time. If you've time right now, I'd like you to come over and tell me what you'll need for your apartment."

She met his gaze with a surprising jolt of trepidation. She'd had the flurry of activity that always came with preparing for the start-up of school to distract her from the decision they'd made yesterday. Now that the other students had all gone home and it was just the four of them standing here on the steps, Elsie was beginning to think maybe she might be in over her head. She knew that God wanted her to take on this task. Still, worry pecked its way into the back of her mind.

She didn't know this man. She didn't know where he came from, who his people were, or what kind of a man he was. Certainly, the fact that he'd brought these children with him rather than leaving them at an orphanage meant something. And John Oliver, a pillar of this community, had hired him on as a foreman for his lumber company. In Elsie's mind that meant he must be a decent man. But was it enough for her to keep her promise to care for Harry and Minnie while he was working? And what of their close proximity to each other? She knew they would be living in the same house, but in separate quarters. Still, perhaps now would be a good time to set some ground rules.

He must have sensed her shift in mood because he said, "You can't back out on our agreement, Miss Mitchell. The children need you."

Minnie sat on the steps by her feet, and Harry was dragging a stick he'd found in the school yard through the dirt. After seeing how withdrawn Minnie was even with her brother by her side, and knowing that poor Harry wanted to make more friends but had loyally stuck by his sister's side all day, Elsie knew in her heart of hearts that she couldn't back out of their agreement.

Quietly, she spoke. "I know they need stability."

"Walk to the house with me so I can show you around. You can look at your accommodations."

"I'll meet you there in half an hour. I have to gather some papers together so I can grade them tonight. As soon as I lock up the building, I'll come over."

He folded his arms across his chest, taking a wide stance with his legs.

She could tell he thought she wouldn't come. "Mr. Benton, I always keep my word. I'll be by, I promise."

"We'll look for you in half an hour, then."

"Yes."

He motioned for the children to join him and then walked away. Elsie was about to start back up the steps when she saw Mr. Craig from the telegraph office come up to Mr. Benton and hand him a piece of paper. He read the paper and then with a nod to Mr. Craig turned to walk home with the children.

Will scanned the telegram and then stuck it in his shirt pocket. He turned, about to ask Miss Mitchell whether Harry and Minnie could stay with her for a bit longer, but she'd gone back inside. Giving a shrug, he thought now would be as good a time as any to look like a family man. With Harry and Minnie in tow, he set out for the other side of the street. Leaving them within eyesight of the swinging doors, he entered the saloon, scanning the room until he saw her.

Busy pouring a glass of whiskey, she pretended not to notice him. He sauntered across the wide-planked floor. Peanut shells crunched beneath his boots. Cigar smoke swirled around him, leaving a haze in his wake. The woman with brilliant red hair in the bright-red dress didn't acknowledge him until he stood in front of her.

The feather in her headband swayed back and forth as she leaned across the bar. "What'll ya have?"

"The usual."

She poured two fingers of whiskey into a short glass and slid it across the bar to him. "You new in town?"

"Sort of," he answered, playing along with the charade. Will scanned the mirror behind her, noticing three men playing cards off in a corner. "I received a message."

Resting her elbows on the bar, she batted her long, dark lashes at him. "Did you now?"

"Come on, Lily, don't hold out on me. Why are you here?" He studied her face, noticing she'd been a bit heavy-handed with the stage makeup. Those pockmarks on her face looked real.

Lily Handland's brown eyes sparkled with mischief.

"It's been a long time since we've worked together, Will. Maybe I needed a change of scenery."

He knew better than to be deceived by the flirtations of the best female Pinkerton in the agency. He brought the glass to his lips, pretending to sip from it, and then set the glass on the bar. In the mirror he watched a man in a black vest and white shirt sit down at the piano. His long fingers wandered over the keys. Tin notes echoed off the walls.

He heard Lily's voice close to his left ear. "Word is your mark is coming here."

"Description?"

"None right now. I'll get word to you if I find out anything more. Just be on the lookout."

He nodded. Holding the glass in his hand, he swirled the amber-colored whiskey. Lily left the bar and sashayed across the room to join the man at the piano.

Elsie set about ending the school day. Returning to the classroom, she paused by the desk that Minnie and Harry had shared. Harry had done very well on his testing. He could actually read out of the third-grade primer. He needed a bit of work on his writing, but Elsie felt that with a little effort there would be improvement.

Realizing it would be impossible for Minnie to read out loud, she'd had her work only on some small arithmetic problems and copy some simple sentences out of the first-grade primer. Minnie tested out a grade level below her brother. Mildly worried, Elsie knew that time and the Lord's helping hand would heal the child. Elsie was hopeful she would catch up by the end of this semester.

She emerged from the building a little over half an hour later. Hating to be even the tiniest bit tardy, and imagining Mr. Benton pacing impatiently in wait of her arrival, she hurried along the planked sidewalk toward the house. She had gone about halfway when a fuss outside the saloon caught her attention. A man wielding a broom came toward two small children on the walkway in front of the building. Raising the broom, he shouted at them.

She immediately recognized the riot of curls flowing down the little girl's back. What on earth were Harry and Minnie doing outside that building? And where was their uncle? Fear pumped through her veins, spurring her forward. She could see Minnie and Harry trying to run away from the man. Minnie cried out as her brother tried to shield her by pushing her behind him.

By the time Elsie got to the building, her fear turned to anger. Drawing in a deep breath, she steeled her shoulders for a fight. It was all she could do to temper her emotion as she made her way to the frightened children. In front of them, the barkeep hoisted the broom handle behind his back, preparing to swat at them. Harry cried out and stumbled.

The noise of men laughing and some of the most dreadful piano music she'd ever heard spilled out onto the street. Hoisting her skirts above her ankles, she rushed up the steps to stand between the children and the horrid man who was missing two front teeth and smelled as if he hadn't taken a bath in quite some time.

With her nose twitching and her heart pounding, Elsie grabbed at the broom handle. "Leave these children alone!"

"They've no business playing here," he replied, then spat a steady stream of murky, vile tobacco juice from between his teeth.

"Oh!" Jumping back in disgust to avoid the brown splatter, and at the same time reaching out to grab the arm of each child, she pulled them up to stand one on each side of her. "You, sir, are disgusting."

"And this is no place for a *lady*." He drew out the word like he believed her to be no such thing, adding, "And those young'uns got to move along."

At least on that she agreed with the wretched man. Looking down at the children, she gazed from one surprised face to the other, demanding, "Where's your uncle William?"

"He's inside," Harry answered, trying to squirm out of her reach.

"Stay still, Harry. You're not the one in trouble. How long have you two been out here?" she asked, quickly looking them over to make certain they were unharmed.

He gave a quick shrug of his little shoulders. "We came here right after we left the school yard."

She forced herself to soften her tone. "What is your uncle thinking? This is no place for children."

"Are you going to yell at Uncle Will?"

Sighing, Elsie fought to rein in her temper. After all, this was not their fault. It was William Benton's, and he was about to be told in no uncertain terms how the saloon entryway was not an appropriate place to leave children. Taking Harry and Minnie by the hand, she walked them to the opposite edge of the boardwalk. "You two stay right here until I come back. Don't move a muscle; don't speak to anyone. Do you understand me?"

Harry's head bobbed up and down. "Yes, Miss Mitchell."

Putting a smile on her face, she added, "After this, I'll take you over to the bakery for a treat. How does that sound?"

Minnie hugged her doll to her chest while Harry beamed. "We'll stay right here, Miss Mitchell. We won't move one bit. Right, Minnie?"

The little girl nodded.

"All right, then. I'll be back in a few minutes."

After straightening her short jacket, she secured her bonnet and marched right up to the swinging shutter doors that led to what was surely Heartston's very own version of Sodom and Gomorrah. Taking a stance a mere inch from the doors, she opened her mouth and, heaven help her, yelled, "William Benton, you get out here right this minute!"

Raucous laughter greeted her demand. A swirl of red and black in the form of a scantily clad saloon girl appeared before her.

"You looking for your man, lady?" The girl's brilliant red hair was adorned with a sequined headband, which had a colorful ostrich feather sticking out from it.

Her face had seen better days. Pockmarks scarred her heavily rouged cheeks. If she were in a better frame of mind, Elsie might have felt sorry for this creature's plight and would be praying for her salvation. Right now, though, she could concentrate only on getting William Benton out here. Feeling as though the entire town were staring at her, Elsie bit back a tart remark as she felt a heated blush spreading across her face like wildfire.

"He's not my man." Forcing herself to remain calm, she said, "I'd be grateful if you could find him and send him out here, please."

The thought of her and Mr. Benton as a couple made her tremble in fury. A man who could abandon children like some animals on the side of a street while he sated his lust would never be the man for her!

The woman disappeared with a rustle of stiff red taffeta. Feeling like she may have gone a bit too far by creating such a scene, Elsie took a step to the side of the door, pulling the wide brim of her bonnet lower. Three men came out the doors before Mr. Benton finally exited. And then he completely ignored her, walking right past her toward the children.

Gathering her skirts, she trudged up right behind him. Her anger was so great that she had to force herself to take a moment to say a silent prayer for calmness. She reminded herself that the children were present. Barely stopping to retrieve his charges, he seemed oblivious to her presence. Lengthening her stride, she matched his pace.

"Mr. Benton! You cannot leave these children on the sidewalk while you do . . ." Sputtering, she searched for the right words. "Whatever it was you were doing back there in that horrible place."

Casting a sidelong glance at him, she saw his back stiffen. He had some nerve being angry at her! Not to be deterred by his silence, Elsie finally caught hold of his arm right above his elbow. Startled by the flexing of firm muscle, she quickly dropped her hand to her side.

"Mr. Benton! Stop!"

"Follow me to my home, Miss Mitchell. We can talk there."

"But Uncle Will, Miss Mitchell promised we could get a bakery treat." Harry's plaintive whine sliced through the tension-filled air.

Mr. Benton glanced at her.

Daring to speak, she said, "I promised them if they behaved while I went to find you that they could have a treat."

Turning away from her, he looked down the street to where the bake shop stood. The wonderful scent of its locally famous cinnamon rolls wafted from the open door all the way to where they stood. Elsie thought it one of the most blessed scents of the entire town. Looking at the hopeful expressions on the children's faces, she hoped Mr. Benton thought so, too.

"All right! I'd hate to make a lady go back on her word."

They drew up short in front of the storefront, where Mr. Benton said, "You will wait here while I go buy the cinnamon rolls." A few minutes later he returned with a full brown paper bag. Handing it to her for safekeeping, he led the way to the opposite end of the town in silence.

She didn't know what to do with his brooding silence. When they finally reached the house, Mr. Benton turned to take the bag from her.

The place looked much better than it had in months. The porch had been swept clean of the dried leaves and twigs left over from the previous fall, the windows had been cleaned of grime, and the front door stood ajar. Pausing at the base of the steps, she watched as the trio disappeared into the house. Putting her hand on the rail, she started up the steps, only to be stopped by Mr. Benton as he returned to the porch.

"The children are washing up." Folding his arms across his chest, he stood looming over her on the top step.

Despite his intimidating stance, she was determined to make him understand that his actions had been completely inappropriate. Removing her hand from the railing, she took a moment to gather her thoughts.

She looked up at him and said, "Mr. Benton, you can't leave children that age unattended! Too many things could happen to them. Strangers come through this town quite frequently on their way to the mountain retreats. There's no telling who these people are, where they came from, or what their intentions might be."

"Don't you think I'm aware of the dangers out in the world?"

"I'm saying that it has become clear to me, sir, that you have no idea how to raise children. They are in need of a great deal of care, the first part of which is seeing they are safe at all times. The saloon. . . ."

She gulped in a breath before continuing, watching as he narrowed his gaze even further at her. "What were you thinking?"

She hadn't intended to ask the question. It just popped out of her mouth on its own volition.

"It's none of your business what I was thinking, Miss Mitchell."

Elsie plowed onward, keeping the children's needs at the forefront of her thoughts. "I was going to take a few days to organize my belongings, but after what I just witnessed, I fear the children might come to harm if I'm not here to ensure their safekeeping."

His face relaxed a fraction, and she thought this might be because he was about to have another person to shoulder some of his parental responsibilities. She soldiered on because there were a few new stipulations to her final acceptance of this job.

"There are things you must agree to before I move into the apartment."

"You promised me back at the school yard that you'd be coming here."

"That was before I found the children, alone, outside the saloon."

They engaged in a silent standoff, until he spoke first. "Go on."

"Dinner will be on the table every night by six o'clock. I will not stay up awaiting your return from your work. Then there is the matter of church services. The children and you will attend them every Sunday. I cannot tolerate a lack of the Lord's guidance in their lives." She noted that with every rule she imparted, his stance had begun to change, until he stood with his feet apart and his arms crossed in front of his chest, squinting at her with an angry glare.

Undeterred by his silent intimidation, she ended with the one thing she felt certain would be like poking a stick into a hornet's nest. "I cannot abide by your visits to the saloon."

Moments passed when the only sound to be heard was the chirping of the spring birds in a nearby budding weeping willow tree.

"While I will try to be here for dinner at the appointed time, you must understand that there will be times when my job will not allow for that. Working at the lumber company does not come with specified hours. I may be required to be up at the lumber camp for days at a time."

"The children and I will deal with those times as they come along. But you mustn't work on the Lord's Day. This will set a terrible example for the children. And frankly, Mr. Benton, from what I've seen today, you are in need of some time with the Lord."

Dropping his arms to his sides, he said, "Miss Mitchell, I'm delighted that you will be helping with Harry and Minnie."

Her mood brightened a bit at his remark. "Thank you." And then it just as quickly plummeted when he held up a hand.

"Let me finish, please."

"Of course. Go on."

"I am a man who has needs."

Her gaze wavered from his as the heat of a blush spread across her face.

"I will go to the saloon when I choose to. And as for my time with the Lord, that is between me and the man up above."

She could learn to tolerate many disagreements, but his choosing not to attend church wasn't one of them. Elsie immediately wanted to rescind her offer to stay and care for the children. She might have done just that if Harry and Minnie hadn't chosen to make an appearance.

Harry awarded her a smile. "Is it true, Miss Mitchell? Are you really going to be staying here with us so soon?"

She didn't answer right away. Her mind was busy formulating a way to get their uncle to see the light of day in regard to the proper rearing of children. Finally, she said, "So long as your uncle agrees to accompany us to church services every Sunday, I'll be here to help take care of you and your sister."

Will was awestruck by the schoolmarm's audacity. How dare she dictate to him the conditions of her employment? He'd known from the start that Miss Mitchell was going to be a stubborn woman. But he'd no idea just how tenacious she could be. Although she didn't know it, the matter of his going to the saloon had nothing to do with his needs as a man or for drinking. Alcohol hadn't passed his lips since he'd started working with the Pinkerton Agency. Truth be told, Will didn't care for the drink.

However, the telegram that had been delivered to him outside the schoolhouse had indicated that the mark could be on the move. Furthermore, there was no changing the ways of certain criminals who made it a habit to haunt such establishments. If the mark was to be found in the saloon, then it was Will's job to follow the lead there. To his way of thinking, the children had been perfectly safe outside the building.

Maybe he'd been wrong about his decision to leave them there. But he'd had to act quickly, and he'd felt sure they'd be all right on the walkway outside the saloon.

"I thought they would be fine. I was keeping an eye on them." Will had seen them through the saloon's swinging doors not five minutes before Miss Mitchell had come along. They'd been fine.

"The children are not dogs, Mr. Benton. They can't be left unattended."

He realized that the children couldn't be taken care of while he worked his cases. And he didn't see them as animals. He'd just put his job first. Miss Mitchell was right, Will had the twins' well-being to consider first now.

On the other hand, the church issue was stuck in Miss Mitchell's craw like honey on a bear's paw. Here she was a professed good Christian woman using the emotions of these innocent children to get her way. Will didn't think that was acting Christian-like at all. He didn't say those words to her, though. He knew she had him over a barrel. He needed her here in order to carry out his current Pinkerton assignment, and as much as he was loath to admit it, he needed her to help keep his cover intact. What better way to keep his mark off track than to look like a lumberjack foreman with a small family?

Will watched the corners of her mouth twitch up in a triumphant smile as she realized he was going to accept her conditions. He had to hand it to her, she knew how to bide her time. But darned if her toe didn't get to a-tapping, giving away her impatience. Leaning against the porch post, he leveled what he knew to be his most intimidating stare— one that had stopped many criminals in their tracks. Her toe stilled.

Satisfied that she knew who was in control here, he said, "If my work allows for it, I will attend your church services."

It was the best he could offer her. It had been a long time since he and the Lord had had much to say to each other. Since it looked like she was going to rebut his counteroffer, he held up his hand to stop her. "That's all you're going to get from me, Miss Mitchell. Take it or leave it."

Raising her chin just a notch, she pinned him with a firm gaze. "I suppose it will have to do. For now."

Shaking his head at her last words, he frowned. He was beginning to wonder if he'd finally met his match.

Chapter Four

Letting out a sigh of pent-up frustration, Elsie gathered her skirts and climbed up the steps past Mr. Benton. Going into the house, she was pleased to find that the rooms had been aired and swept out. Walking through the parlor, she followed the sound of Harry's voice. Passing through a side door, she discovered a good-sized cooking area. There was a cast-iron cook stove and a sink along one wall; a hand-hewn table sat in the middle of the room with two benches tucked underneath. The children stood in front of the sink. Harry was helping his sister dry her hands on a worn dish towel.

"Miss Mitchell, isn't this house nice?"

"From what I've seen of it, yes it is, Harry." Smiling at them, she wandered over to inspect the sink. She was relieved to find it clean. The floorboards creaked behind her, and she turned to find William Benton standing in the doorway.

"Why don't I give everyone a tour?"

"That would be lovely. Come on, children, let's take a look at our new home." The phrase "our new home" sounded strange and had Elsie wondering once again whether she'd gotten in way over her head. She took a moment to remind herself of the prayers she'd prayed, renewing her purpose for being here. This was what she was meant to be doing.

Mr. Benton allowed her and the children to precede him up the staircase in the center of the house. She noticed the faint, worn remnants of a leaf pattern adorning the stairwell and thought that Mr. Oliver's grandmother might have hired an itinerant artist to do the work. Even though the paint was aged, it still had a remarkable patina to it. The late-afternoon sunlight bounced off the hall walls. Mr. Benton pointed to the first room on the right.

"I thought I'd make this my room, and then Minnie and Harry could have their pick of the other two bedrooms. Or they could share the one across the hall from mine."

Out of the corner of her eye, she saw Minnie grab hold of her brother's hand.

"I think it might be a good idea to put them in the same room for now. I don't have any siblings, but I imagine it would be fun to share a room with one." Minnie shot her a look, and Elsie thought she saw some of the wariness fade from the little girl's eyes.

Looking into the room directly across the hall from where Mr. Benton would be sleeping, she said, "The bed looks to be large enough for both of them. So after supper, we'll do our best to freshen the room."

Though she knew he'd worked hard to air out the house, there hadn't been time to wash the bed linens. She made a mental note to put that at the top of her chore list. If the weather held, she might be able to get this done within the next few days.

Mr. Benton allowed her to go down the hallway and peek into the last room on this floor. It contained two small beds and a nightstand. They made their way back downstairs.

"I'd like to see my quarters now, if that's all right with you."

"Of course. Your entrance is right off the kitchen."

Again she followed him, the children in their wake. After a cursory look around the sitting area, where a potbelly stove stood in one corner, and then the bedroom, with a suitable bed and a lovely window that looked out to a side yard, she was surprised to find a small washroom. She remembered that as Mr. Oliver's grandmother had gotten on in years, the stairs had become too much for her and he had added some of these conveniences for her.

Looking at the cobwebs hanging in the crevices of the small room, and adding their removal to the mental list she'd been keeping track of, Elsie realized she had her work cut out for her. Not only would she be putting together lesson plans for her students, but she would be setting this household to rights.

A wagon rattled near the house and creaked to a halt. Mr. Benton excused himself and left her there with the children. "I think we might have our first visitor. Shall we go see who is here?"

Minnie hugged her doll and held on to Harry's hand as they walked to the front entry. The door stood open. To Elsie's delight, the wagon was bearing what looked to be a load of supplies. Leaving the children safely in the parlor, she went out to assist with the unloading. A cool breeze came across the porch, ruffling her skirts. Shivering, she pulled the shawl around her shoulders.

"You can wait inside with the children, Miss Mitchell. I can handle this," Mr. Benton said.

"I'm fine. More hands will make the job go faster. It looks to me like you bought out most of the mercantile!" She smiled up at him.

"The house needs most everything to be up and running. Why don't you take this box here? There should be something in there to make into a supper. You do that, and I'll see to the rest of it."

Taking the box from him, she went back into the house and set the contents on the table. She found the makings for a hearty soup. While Mr. Benton brought box after box of stock into the kitchen, she chopped up some root vegetables and tossed them into the cast-iron pot on the back of the stove. After stirring the embers in the firebox, she added a few pieces of wood. As the fire burned hot, she walked back to the sink and worked the pump until the cold well water flowed.

Taking a tin pitcher from the back of the sink, she filled it, then added the water to the soup pot. She placed a lid on the pot, allowing it to simmer. Soon the house was filled with the comforting smells of a good dinner.

While the children played outside on the porch, she and Mr. Benton worked in silence, setting canned goods and sacks of flour, rice, and sugar on the shelves lining the back wall of the kitchen.

Elsie went to the stove and, picking up a large spoon, tended to the pot, saying, "I know I said I'd stay on right away, but I'll need to go back to my parents' house to pack up my belongings. So if it's all right with you, I will go home tonight, and then I'll have my father bring me into town tomorrow morning so we can leave my belongings here."

"That sounds like a good idea. I'm sure the children will be fine spending one more night alone with me."

Elsie couldn't help feeling that her life was taking a turn. Walking to the window, she looked out to watch Minnie and Harry playing on the porch. Already they looked happier. The sight lifted her heart.

Turning away, she asked, "Where are the eating utensils?"

"I saw some in the cabinet by the door." Mr. Benton opened the cabinet and took out four white bowls, and after some rifling around, he also pulled out spoons.

Elsie took one look at the thick layer of grime covering them and said, "These are filthy." She scrubbed them in the sink until they were cleaned to her satisfaction, then set them out on the table.

Pausing in the chore, she looked to where Mr. Benton stood in the doorway. "There's no need for you to help me with the cooking."

"Just trying to be helpful, ma'am."

"I appreciate that. But I don't want you thinking I can't handle these responsibilities."

"I didn't think that at all. I'll stay out of your way from here on out."

Fearing she might have insulted him, Elsie quickly added, "It's not that you can't be in here. I just want you to understand that I can handle preparing the meals."

The issue settled, she went to the front door, opened it, and beckoned the children inside to eat. When Harry made a beeline for a seat at the table, she softly scolded him. "We must wash our hands before we eat, Harry."

"But Miss Mitchell, we just did that."

"I know. But we walked around the house, and you and your sister have been playing outside. It never hurts to have clean hands." Ushering them to the sink, Elsie pumped a small bit of water. Finishing up, they each found a place at the table.

When everyone had settled, she said, "Let's say a prayer of thanksgiving for our supper."

Remembering their earlier conversation concerning the Lord, she dared to glance across the table to where Mr. Benton sat opposite her. He was watching her with those dark eyes. A feeling of trepidation skittered down her spine. She felt certain he would set a good example for his niece and nephew. Then again, he was used to being out on his own in a world where she felt certain the boundaries of decency were few and far between.

She noticed he still wore his hat. Trying not to make a spectacle out of the fact, she raised her eyes, inclining her head in his direction.

Immediately reading her expression, he removed the hat, hanging it off the back of his chair. She folded her hands, waiting while the children mimicked her actions. Looking down the length of the table, she noticed his were resting alongside the soup bowl. Silence descended upon them. Again she met his gaze. A good minute ticked by before he followed suit. Bending her head, she decided to keep her words simple. "Lord, we thank you for putting a roof over our heads and for the nourishment of this meal. As always, we welcome your guidance in our lives. Amen."

Even before she opened her eyes and lifted her head, Elsie felt Mr. Benton's gaze upon her. And when she returned his look with an unwavering one of her own, she saw the wariness reflected in his eyes. As far as she was concerned, the man was just going to have to get used to the fact that she would be not only bringing stability to this little family but also sharing her faith, too.

After they finished up their meal and cleaned up the dishes, Mr. Benton loaded her and the children into a borrowed wagon and drove her out to her parents' house. She assured the children that this would be her last night apart from them, then bid them good night.

Will walked Miss Mitchell to the doorstep of her parents' home. Before he could step away, the door opened, revealing a tall man with similar features to Miss Mitchell.

"Good evening, Elsie."

"Father!" She sounded surprised to see him. "Mr. Benton was kind enough to bring me home." Watching them, she fidgeted with the strings of her reticule.

A woman whom Will assumed from the violet color of her eyes to be Elsie's mother came to join them.

"Mother, Father, this is William Benton, the man whose niece and nephew I'll be caring for."

Eventually, Mr. Benton put out his hand and her father shook it. Then he tipped his hat to Elsie's mother. "Pleasure to meet you both."

Will thought perhaps Elsie's parents might want to know more about the position offered to their daughter. Instead, Mr. Mitchell said, "Thank you for seeing our daughter home."

Taking Elsie by the elbow, he ushered her inside the house.

Mr. Mitchell's attitude might be polite, but it was not welcoming. Will knew it was best to leave Miss Mitchell to deal with her parents. Nodding in the direction of the wagon, he said, "It's getting late. I need to get the children back to town."

He climbed back onto the buckboard to find Minnie sucking her thumb and Harry fidgeting on the seat next to her. For the majority of the ride back to town, Harry complained about having to leave Miss Mitchell behind.

"Uncle Will, why couldn't she stay with us tonight?"

"Harry, I told you already, Miss Mitchell needs to gather her belongings." Rolling his shoulders, Will realized he felt Harry's frustration and then some. But there wasn't much to be done about the fact that the schoolteacher's relocation couldn't happen tonight, so he urged the horse along, making a quick trip back to Heartston.

After leaving the wagon at the stable, he carried a half-asleep Minnie back to the Oliver house. Harry insisted on dragging his feet, making Will impatient.

"Harry, I need you to keep up with me."

"I'm tired," he complained, bumping into Will's leg.

Blowing out a breath, Will forced himself to slow to Harry's pace. "We're almost to the house now."

Within minutes they were climbing the steps to the front porch. Opening the front door, Will set Minnie down inside the parlor. He waited for Harry to join them, then firmly closed the door behind them all.

"Let's get settled for the night." Ushering them up the stairs to the second floor, Will attempted to lead them into the room he and Miss Mitchell had decided would be the most suitable for the children. But it seemed both of them had other plans.

"We don't want to sleep in there, Uncle Will. Minnie is afraid of the dark."

"You were perfectly fine last night in the room we slept in."

"That's because you were with us in the same room, Uncle Will."

Stepping into the room where the bed had been made up earlier by Miss Mitchell, Will found a lamp on the dresser and, striking a match, lit it, setting the flame to high. The light cast long shadows into the room. Minnie latched on to his pant leg, trembling.

"Look, you'll be fine in here. I'll be right across the hallway if you need anything. I promise I'll hear you if you call out."

Harry shook his head while Minnie sucked her thumb. Will wasn't cut out for parenthood. He'd never wanted to be a father. He was a loner. It was the reason he made a good Pinkerton agent; he had no one waiting for him, depending on him to return. Looking up at the ceiling, he wondered what he was supposed to do with the children. They needed to get some sleep. He also needed to get a decent night's rest.

Doing the only thing he could think of, Will led them across the hallway to his bedroom. "Get yourselves up in that bed," he said, unable to keep the gruffness out of his voice.

Harry sent him a small, grateful smile while Minnie picked the right side of the bed—his side of the bed—and made herself right at home, snuggling into what was to be his pillow. As they made themselves comfortable, Will sat at the foot of the bed, the mattress giving under his weight.

"You could sleep between us," Harry suggested.

Will tossed a doubtful look at the boy. "Harry, last night you and your sister slept without me. Why do you need me near you now?"

His reply came as a frightened whisper. "This is a big house, and there are a lot of noises."

Giving in would set a bad precedent. But sharing his bed for one night probably wouldn't hurt. He just had to be clear with Harry.

"All right, but only for tonight. When Miss Mitchell arrives tomorrow, you and Minnie will go back across the hallway."

Harry nodded.

Will tugged off his boots, set them on the floor next to the foot of the bed, and then climbed in. It didn't take long for the children to snuggle up against him. Will kept his arms to his sides, but before long, Minnie's small head rested on his shoulder and Harry's slight form curled underneath one of his arms. Will lay very still, counting the hours until Miss Mitchell returned.

Chapter Five

The next day Elsie's father helped her load a trunkful of her belongings onto his wagon. Her mother stood beside the wagon, gripping the edge of the white apron she wore over her dress. There hadn't been any discussion after Mr. Benton dropped her off last night. Her father had taken his Bible into the back bedroom. When Elsie tried to broach the subject of the children, her mother had told her they would pray on it and discuss the matter in the morning.

"It was kind of Mr. Benton to bring you home last night," her mother said. "Although with the lateness of the hour . . . those children should have been getting ready for bed."

Elsie heard the disapproving tone in her mother's voice. She defended his actions. "As I've told you, there is no one else to help with them."

The sun crested the rise at the far side of her father's property. One of the first rays of sunlight rested on them, warming her skin. Her father spoke, his deep, rumbling voice giving Elsie comfort, reminding her why she loved listening to him read their nightly Bible verses.

"I know you're headstrong. From the time you were a young girl, you've always had an independent nature. But this is not your family, Elsie. You don't have to take on this responsibility."

His words were nothing she hadn't thought about already. "Harry and Minnie are orphans. They've no control over their circumstances. Their uncle is trying to do what's right by them."

"Does the answer to his prayers have to be you, Elsie?" he asked.

"Psalm 127 talks about children being a heritage from the Lord. And you know there are many more verses about taking in orphans," she said quietly to prove her case. "I met Mr. Benton and those children for a reason. Let me try to help them."

"I know you're going to go live with them no matter what I say."

"Father, it would be so much easier if I had your blessing."

He was silent for a moment and then said, "Let us join hands in prayer."

The trio formed a small circle alongside the wagon. His voice carried softly on the breeze. "Heavenly Father, I beseech you to guide Elsie as she begins yet another new journey in her life. Keep her safe and help her to make a warm and loving home for Harry and Minnie. Guide me so I can guide my daughter. Amen."

Elsie and her mother followed with amens of their own. Her father came to her and took her hands in his strong grip.

"Right now I'm only giving you my half blessing." He smiled down at her. "I love you and only want you to be happy. But you must know this isn't what I think is best for you."

She nodded, thankful her father was going to let her go. "I understand, Father. Thank you."

Smiling, Elsie went to give her mother a hug. Holding her mother close, she said, "Don't worry about me. I'll be fine."

"I know. You're my brave girl."

Releasing her mother, she hoisted herself up onto the wagon seat. The ride to town proved to be uneventful. When her father started to head toward the Oliver house, Elsie informed him, "I'll get off at the bakery. I need to speak with Amy."

Abiding by her wishes, her father changed course, eventually stopping the wagon in front of the bake shop. Resting the leather reins loosely between his fingers, he turned to her. "Elsie, I know you want to help this family, but if you are for one second not comfortable there, for any reason, you bring those children and yourself back home."

"Papa, this is what I'm supposed to be doing." Tapping her chest lightly, she added, "My heart is telling me that helping out this man and those children is right." She gave him a quick hug and departed the wagon. She saw the doubt reflected in his light-blue eyes, but bravely she waved him off.

Gathering her skirts, she stepped onto the wooden walkway in front of Amy's. Peering into the steamy window pane, she saw her friend standing behind the counter, putting this morning's freshly baked cinnamon rolls on a large tray. Amy saw her and waved her in, her blue eyes sparkling.

"Good morning, Amy!"

"Elsie! I was hoping you'd find some time to stop by. I've missed you." Brushing the flour from her hands, she came around the counter to pull Elsie into a warm embrace. "I'm so happy you've returned," she whispered.

"I'm glad to be back. I've so much to tell you."

"How about some tea?"

"Tea would be wonderful. To be truthful, I had to be up before the crack of dawn this morning and I didn't have time for breakfast."

She followed Amy through to the room where all the wonderful confections were lovingly mixed and baked.

Taking a teapot and matching cups with saucers down from the shelf over the sink, Amy set them on top of a small table situated in the far corner of the room. She measured some tea leaves into the pot and then filled it from a kettle on the stove.

"Is it true what I've been hearing? That you're moving into John Oliver's grandmother's old house?"

Living in a small town, Elsie knew it was impossible to keep something like this a secret, and yet she was still surprised by how quickly the news had reached her friend. She wished she had made the time to tell her herself.

"It is and I am. Actually, that's the reason I'm here so early." When Amy frowned at her, she quickly added, "I'm going to be helping Mr. William Benton care for his niece and nephew. They were recently orphaned. He came to town to take a job at the Oliver Lumber Company."

"Those poor children!"

"They've been through a very difficult time. They need someone to help care for them. I'll have my own apartment. It's situated off the kitchen," she explained. Then it dawned on her that perhaps Amy might be upset because she would no longer have the time to help out at the bakery. "Amy, I'm so sorry. I do appreciate your offer to let me come work here."

"Don't worry about that. I can find a replacement for you," she replied. Walking over to the sideboard, she put some lemon-drop cookies on a small plate. Bringing them back to the table, she offered one to Elsie. "I'm worried about you. First you leave on this trip to Albany, and then you're not even back here for two days and you're moving in with this family."

Elsie knew that Amy had her best interests at heart and wasn't trying to be critical, yet somehow she felt that her friend thought she might be acting impulsively.

"By doing this, I'm killing two birds with one stone. Mr. Benton desperately needs someone to help with the children, and I'm earning extra money." She left out her plans to one day soon be able to afford to travel on a ship. Amy didn't always approve of her wanderlust, so she added, "Mr. Oliver gave a good argument as to why this arrangement would work out."

"John Oliver was involved in this?" Amy raised her pale eyebrows in surprise.

Elsie sipped at the tea, noticing the light blush on her friend's face. Amy had been smitten with that man for months.

"You could say he orchestrated the entire thing. He had us come to his office practically the moment we stepped off the train. He knows how much I want to plan my next trip and is aware of what my teacher's salary is. It's really little more than a stipend. Not that I'm complaining, mind you."

Amy smiled and said, "It's a good thing you're devoted to the cause of educating Heartston's children."

"The proper education of those children is my life," she replied.

"You are the best teacher this town has ever had. Enough about this. I want to hear about your trip to Albany. You must have gone to dinners and had afternoon teas!"

"I went to one of the finest tearooms. It was on Ogdon Street in a lovely establishment. We had cucumber sandwiches with watercress, and some of the slices of bread even had smoked fish."

"I'd love to have a tearoom here. I know they have afternoon teas over at the Great Camps on Blue Mountain Lake every Sunday. I don't think Heartston would have enough people to support one, though. All those lumberjacks prefer the saloon." Elsie fought back a scowl as she thought about finding Mr. Benton there yesterday. It was a good thing she'd seen the children when she did. Lord only knew the harm that might have come to them.

"Maybe we could go over to one of the afternoon teas?" Amy was still talking about tearooms. "We could get all dressed up in our best finery and maybe find a gentleman or two to accompany us."

"Ha! Do you think any of these lumberjacks would even have proper clothing? Besides which, most of them are so exhausted by the time Sunday comes around that they end up sleeping the day away." All this talk was nothing more than wishful thinking. Elsie feared she'd be so busy getting the Benton household in order over the coming days, there would be little free time.

"Perhaps I could convince John Oliver to accompany me." Amy cast a wistful look toward the building across the street.

"And here I thought you'd forgotten all about him," Elsie said, teasing her friend.

"How can I forget about him when I see him nearly every day? Most mornings he drops in for one of my muffins."

"Maybe one day you'll ask him to stay for tea." Her comment brought another fresh blush to Amy's cheeks.

"Tell me some more about your trip," Amy said, clearly changing the subject. "You know I never get to leave here, and I love listening to your adventures."

Last year, Amy's parents had taken her younger brother and sister and gone to Connecticut to live. Her mother's sister had been ailing for some time and needed help. Amy hadn't wanted to leave her life here in Heartston and had convinced her family that she could keep the bakery going until their return. This left Amy to run the bake shop on her own. It also left her with little free time.

Elsie had thought about not telling anyone about her run-in with her former fiancé, Virgil Jensen. But Amy would know exactly what to make of his actions. So, after nibbling on a bit of a cookie, she swallowed and began her tale.

"Two weeks ago, the day after I arrived in Albany, Aunt Olga and Uncle George took me to dinner at this delightful restaurant situated on the Hudson River. We were in the middle of our second course, oysters on a half shell—"

Amy interrupted. "They sound like they tasted heavenly."

"The oysters were dressed with a spicy bit of red sauce, like nothing I've ever tasted before. But it's the usual fare for them on a Friday evening."

"This sounds so glamorous compared to Heartston."

"Don't get all dreamy-eyed, Amy. Too much rich food is not good for the digestion, I'm afraid." Elsie left it to Amy's imagination. "City life is so different from ours here in the country. The air is quite dirty from all the factories. I missed the trees and I missed all of my students."

"They were all right here where you left them. I'm sensing something happened while you were at this dinner."

"Yes." She moved to the edge of her chair, leaning toward Amy. She lowered her voice, saying, "We were right in the middle of our oysters when Virgil Jensen showed up at our table."

Coughing on the tea she'd just swallowed, Amy drew in a breath and sputtered, "*The* Virgil Jensen? Your former betrothed?"

"Yes. The very same. He was the last person I expected to see while on holiday."

"How did he look?"

"He looked horrible. A shell of the man he once was."

A small gasp escaped Amy.

Elsie nodded, still feeling much the same shock at his condition. "He is rail thin, with long, unkempt hair. Remember how he always prided himself on his appearance? I don't think he'd bathed in weeks. Frankly, I'm not even certain how he was allowed into the establishment."

Amy wrinkled her nose. "What did he say to you?"

"He asked how I was faring and if I still taught school." She reached for another lemon cookie before continuing. "Then he asked if he could call on me at my aunt and uncle's house."

"I hope you told him no. I for one haven't forgotten how he just up and left you after proposing, leaving you so heartbroken."

Waving a hand in the air, Elsie tried to appear indifferent to Amy's comment. The truth was she had been shattered when Virgil left her. She'd thought she'd found the man of her dreams, one who would take care of her, provide a nice home, and give her children. But that hadn't happened. Virgil Jensen had been her betrothed one day, and the very next day he was gone.

She hated remembering how it had been to pick up the pieces of her heart, to be forced to carry on, going about her teaching job and being in public when everyone in Heartston knew how she'd been deceived. But she'd carried her head high and persevered, somehow surviving the embarrassment and the hurt of his betrayal.

"Elsie? Did you see him again?"

She nodded, eliciting another gasp from Amy. "He came by the very next day. I couldn't just turn him away." She paused, deciding to voice her concerns. "Amy, I fear there is something dark going on inside of him. He's not the same man I knew. The look he gave me when he asked me to carry a packet back to Heartston for him, it was as if he were battling some sort of demons." A shiver went through her as she remembered. "I know this sounds ridiculous, but I felt I had to help him. I told him I'd bring the packet here and put it in safekeeping for him. Now I'm not sure I did the right thing."

"You did what you thought you had to do. Elsie, I've never known you to turn away a person in need. Tell me, what was inside the packet?"

"I never looked."

"What do you think is in it?"

"I don't know. I can only imagine something important. Otherwise, Virgil wouldn't have given it to me."

"Where is it now?"

"I left it at my parents' house."

"Do you think he'll come back for it?"

Elsie sighed. "I don't know."

"About your living arrangements with Mr. Benton and the children," Amy said. "Elsie, are you certain this is what you want to be doing?"

"I am. From the first time I saw them standing on the platform at the train station in Albany, I could tell something wasn't right. I probably wouldn't have even noticed them if my trunk hadn't fallen from the porter's wagon! There I was, standing with my clothing strewn at my feet! Their uncle came to my aid." She felt her face burning as she thought about how he'd handled her delicates.

Across from her, Amy chuckled. "Let me guess, you had some of your silk stockings in the trunk and this Mr. Benton saw them."

"Worse. He picked them up and handed them to me." Shaking a finger at the grin on Amy's face, she scolded, "This is not funny!"

"I'm so sorry . . . Elsie, I've seen your chemises and know about your fondness for those silk stockings." She managed to stifle the next giggle.

Leaning in close, Elsie lowered her voice even though there was no one else in the shop at this hour. "It isn't proper for a gentleman to see a lady's unmentionables. Or have you forgotten your manners, Amy?"

Wiping her eyes, Amy shook her head, her blue eyes sparkling with mischief. "The image of you and Mr. Benton together picking up your *unmentionables*."

"You wouldn't find the situation funny if it had been you, Miss Amy Montgomery!"

Remembering the incident set Elsie to blushing again. The man's grin had told her he liked what he saw. For all her innocence, she recognized desire when she saw it. She imagined he was the sort of man who could have a woman swooning at his feet with just a glance. Elsie wished she could say she'd been immune to his look, but that would be a lie. The minute he'd picked up her stockings and looked at her with those dark eyes, she'd felt something akin to a storm brewing in the pit of her stomach.

And now she'd agreed to reside in the same house with him and the children. The children needed her. No matter what, deep in her heart, she knew her thoughts and actions were for the benefit of Minnie and Harry. *They needed her.* Even if she did feel the slightest bit of interest in their uncle, she would keep her distance from Mr. Benton. To Amy she said, "I've prayed hard about this family, and I feel the Lord wants me to be with them."

Amy reached across the table, patting her hand. "Then that is where you should be. You also need to be honest with yourself. Are you sure there isn't something else going on?"

"What do you mean?"

"I mean are you attracted to Mr. Benton?"

She shook her head. She wouldn't let herself think about the man as anything other than the children's uncle. "Don't be silly, Amy. I'm only there to help with Harry and Minnie."

Amy began to clear up their dishes. "So where does this leave you and Mr. Jensen?"

"I'm going to continue to keep him in my prayers. I fear he's fallen on some very hard times. And I suppose I'll keep his packet in a safe place until he comes for it."

The bell above the bake shop's door rang as a customer entered. Elsie caught the way Amy checked her hair, then quickly changed her dust-covered apron for a clean one.

She saw John Oliver striding over to the service counter. Taking the dishes from her, Elsie nudged her arm with an elbow. "You go on and take care of him. I can see to the dishes."

Pulling her into a quick hug, Amy thanked her.

After clearing their tea service, Elsie walked out from the back room and Mr. Oliver bid her good morning.

"I hope you found the apartment to your liking."

"I did. My father helped me bring my things over earlier this morning."

"Good. I'm pleased everything is going to work out for you and Will."

Anxious to see how Minnie and Harry had fared last night, she gathered her things. The wall clock struck eight times. "Oh dear! Look how the time is getting on. I have to go open up the schoolhouse. Thank you again for tea, Amy."

Chapter Six

Stepping outside, Elsie was hailed by the town's postmaster, Avery Scott, a short, balding, bespectacled man. Crossing the street to see what all his fuss was about, Elsie said, "Good morning, Mr. Scott. It looks like it's going to be a fine day!"

"Indeed." Stepping aside, he held the door open. She entered the post office ahead of him. The small office was located in the front portion of a two-story building. The Scott family occupied the back and upstairs of the rest of the house.

She heard the scurrying of feet above her head and tilted her head toward the ceiling. "I hope this means the children are excited to come to school today?"

Mr. Scott appeared embarrassed that the family's noises could be heard in the office. "With you as their teacher, my children are always happy to go to school. Although Avery Jr. has been putting up a bit of fuss this morning."

"I'm sure he'll be fine once he gets settled at his desk. So, why did you beckon me over here?" She hoped it was because the travel book she'd been waiting weeks for had finally arrived.

He picked up a good-sized package from his desk and handed it to her. "I found this in this morning's mailbag."

She took a look at the return address, pleased to see "Hardy Publishing, New York, New York" in neat block print. "Thank you, Mr. Scott! This is exactly what I've been waiting for."

"I see it's from a New York publisher. Another schoolbook perhaps?"

"A very important one." Gathering the book in her arms, she all but hugged it. "I must be going. Thank you again."

Bounding out the door, she hurried on to the schoolhouse, anxious to take the book out of the package. After unlocking the schoolhouse and setting the precious cargo on her desk, she made her way over to the potbellied stove to start the fire. Once she was sure it would take, she hurried to get the room ready for the day, leaving a few extra minutes before the students started arriving.

Going back to her desk, she carefully unwrapped the brown paper on her package, revealing the small leather-bound book. She ran her fingers over the embossed cover, following the indents of the title, *The Smithson Travel Guide*. It was touted to be the most comprehensive travel guide available, and Elsie hoped the money she'd spent was worth it.

As though holding the Good Book itself, she gingerly opened the cover, eager to get lost in the contents. She smelled the newly printed pages. Running a finger along the first few pages and seeing the chapter titles, she began to imagine all the wonderful lessons the students would get from this book. The excited chattering of their voices interrupted her thoughts.

Closing the book, she left it in the center of her desk and went to greet the first arrivals. Half an hour later the classroom had filled, with the exception of the last two seats in the front row.

Harry's and Minnie's.

Checking her timepiece, she saw it was a quarter past nine. They were running fifteen minutes late. No need to be too worried yet. As she made her way over to where Mr. Scott's eldest child sat, she imagined they were not yet used to waking up in their new home.

"Good morning, Avery."

Bright blue eyes blinked up at her. "Good morning, Miss Mitchell." He squirmed a bit in his seat. His hand quickly covered a sheet of paper with what looked to be the arithmetic problems she'd given to him yesterday to work on at home.

"Avery, is there something you'd like to tell me?"

"No, ma'am."

Deciding to leave it at that, though she suspected Avery was trying to finish his assignment at the last minute, Elsie instructed the children to open their reading primers. She heard the squeak of buggy wheels and glanced toward the doorway expectantly. When the buggy continued on and Minnie and Harry still hadn't appeared, she focused on the class, helping several of the younger students with deciphering some of the harder words.

While the students at the higher level took turns reading aloud from their books, she checked her timepiece to find that another half hour had slipped by. *What's happened to Minnie and Harry?* Fretful, she walked to the window facing the roadway and looked out. She found no sign of them.

Had Mr. Benton been called to work and left the children to fend for themselves again? The memory of finding them outside the saloon haunted her. Elsie's stomach started churning at the thought of those precious ones alone. If they didn't appear soon, she would ask Amy to watch her students while she went to find them.

"Miss Mitchell. Avery is tearing up his paper."

Spinning around, she saw the young man crumpling and tearing at his homework. "Avery! Stop that this instant!" She rushed over to his desk. "Why are you tearing up your work?"

Tears welled in his eyes. Kneeling next to him, she placed her hand on his fingers. Speaking softly, she asked, "Avery, what's all this about?"

"I couldn't decipher the problems you gave me." His lower lip trembled.

"Tearing up your work isn't going to make it go away, Avery. You come to my desk at lunch time and we'll work on them together."

Standing, she glanced at her timepiece again. *Where are those children?* She looked around the room for a student who could be trusted to watch over the classroom until Amy could arrive. She was approaching her oldest student, thirteen-year-old Maggie Wills, when she heard Harry's voice.

"Miss Mitchell!"

Relief flooded through her as the twins entered the room. She tried not to focus on their appearance. Harry's hair was a bit mussed, and his shirttail stuck out every which way through his suspenders. Sweet Minnie wore a wrinkled pinafore over a bright-yellow calico dress. She clutched her doll close to her.

Mr. Benton stood behind the children. Elsie couldn't decide whether the look he wore on his face was one of determination or anger. Perhaps he expected her to criticize the way the children looked or to admonish him for their tardiness. On the contrary, Elsie was just relieved and happy to see them.

"Good morning, ma'am." He tipped his hat. "I apologize for being so late getting Harry and Minnie to school."

"Good morning, Mr. Benton. I'm glad they're here." When Harry made a move to go around her into the schoolroom, Elsie caught him by the arm. Quickly, she straightened his shirttail, tucking it into his pants. Doing her best to smooth Harry's hair, she said to Mr. Benton, "I take it the children spent a restful first night in their new home?" She caught the pained look on his face.

"Um. They didn't exactly take too kindly to sleeping in the room you set up for them."

Harry began to squirm, and she placed a hand on his shoulder to still him. Upon closer inspection, Elsie took in the dark circles under

Mr. Benton's eyes. His clothing was looking a bit rumpled as well. And she thought she heard a rumble of hunger coming from the vicinity of his stomach. She released her hold on Harry.

"Take your sister inside to your seats," she told Harry. *What on earth is going on with this family?* She wished she understood.

Will had honestly done the best he could. Last night had been a nightmare. Even though he'd told Harry and Minnie he would leave a lamp burning low throughout the night, they'd insisted on being with him in his bedroom.

Though Will had tried to accommodate the children, Harry liked to sleep lengthwise across the bed, and Minnie was a tosser and turner. That child hadn't held still for more than five minutes, leaving Will to get short segments of sleep punctuated by either a foot or a hand poking him awake. He felt like he'd been in a saloon fight. Battered and sore, he'd somehow managed to get everyone washed and dressed this morning—two hours late—only to find out that the stove had gone out during the night and he didn't have time to restart it and get their breakfast porridge cooked.

After a few minutes of poking around through their food supplies, he'd found a jar of jam and a package of crackers. That was what he'd given the children for their meal. No complaints from them, but he found that preparing their breakfast and fixing their midday meal didn't leave him time to see to his own needs. So now he stood before the formidable schoolteacher with his stomach growling like a tom cat.

"It appears you've had yourself a rough go of it."

"Let's just say I'm happy you'll be joining us later." Looking beyond her shoulder for a moment, he gathered his thoughts. "I saw your father this morning. He didn't seem too pleased with our arrangement."

"I explained to him that the children need me. He knows I'll be staying in a separate apartment."

"Miss Mitchell, I understand how a man wants to protect his children, especially a daughter. The last thing I want is for your decision to cause problems for you and your family."

"Don't worry about my father. I'm sure he'll come around."

Since she seemed mighty sure of those words, Will decided not to argue the point. If there was one thing he'd learned about the school-teacher, it was that she presented herself as a very confident young woman. But then again, she'd have to be in order for her to have agreed to take on his little family.

"I really shouldn't leave my students alone much longer."

"I'll see you back at the house."

"Yes. If you can leave a low fire in the cook stove, I can put together a proper dinner."

Will didn't know what to make of having someone cook him a proper meal. He worried that Miss Mitchell might be too exhausted after dealing with a room full of children all day long. The last thing he wanted was for her to take on too much.

"We could eat at the hotel dining room."

"Wasn't my meal last night good? You ate every bit of it."

"Your soup was the best meal I've had in ages, ma'am. I thought you might be tired after putting in a long day with the children, that's all."

"Don't worry about me, Mr. Benton. I'll have supper on the table by six o'clock."

"It's settled, then." Tipping his hat to her again, he said, "I'll make sure the cook stove is ready for you." All this talk of food set Will's stomach to growling again. "Have a good day."

"You, too, Mr. Benton."

He watched as she turned and walked back to her students, thinking he'd best be getting back to the house to clean up. Miss Mitchell had no idea how inept he was at running a household. What would she think of him if she could see the mess he'd left the house in? He passed by the saloon and the small post office. A gentle breeze carried the sweet smells of springtime and the savory, mouthwatering scent of the bakeshop's famous cinnamon rolls.

He made a beeline for the bakery, walking right up to the counter to place his order. The owner of the shop greeted him with a shy smile.

"Good morning, Miss Montgomery. I'll take one of your delicious cinnamon rolls, please." Seeing the row of freshly baked bread resting on the countertop behind her, he added, "And a loaf of that fine-looking bread."

He waited while she wrapped up his order.

"I hear that my friend Elsie is going to be helping you out with your family."

He sensed a bit of trepidation coming from Elsie's friend. He wanted to reassure Miss Montgomery that he needed Miss Mitchell, plain and simple. There was nothing more to this arrangement than a business deal. He was paying her more than a fair wage, and he'd be willing to bet she was putting every last cent of those earnings toward her travel fund.

"Mr. Benton?"

"Yes?"

"Elsie is a kind woman who has a big heart. What I'm trying to say is, she's just gotten over a broken engagement."

Suddenly, Will knew exactly what Amy feared. He had no intention of having a relationship beyond that of employer-employee with Elsie Mitchell. His life was complicated enough at the moment.

"I can assure you, you've nothing to worry about as far as Miss Mitchell and I are concerned."

"I'm pleased to hear you say that."

Collecting his order, he bid her a good day.

Walking along the street again, Will realized that even though this town was small by his standards, it was one filled with activity.

71

The saloon was the only place in town that wasn't awake at this hour. Remembering how angry Miss Mitchell had been with him yesterday, he thought it best to keep his distance from the establishment for now. He would find other avenues of pursuing his quarry.

Francis Moore sat in a rocker outside his dry-goods store. His round, ruddy face burst into a broad grin when he spotted Will. "Howdy, Mr. Benton!" Indicating the empty rocker next to him, he invited, "Come, sit down. Take a load off."

Will stepped up onto the narrow walkway. "Don't mind if I do." He sat and then asked, "Having a slow day, are you?"

"Nah. The missus is inside rearranging the sewing notions. It's best I stay out of her way." The man nudged him in the side with his elbow. "I snuck out."

Will laughed. "Smart man."

"You getting settled in?"

"We are."

"That schoolmarm's a fine young woman. She'll be a big help for your children."

Cocking an eyebrow, Will turned to look at the man.

"Told you I know most everything that goes on in this town. Folks don't just come in here to buy from me. We chat. Being friendly is good for business."

Will pondered his statement. He'd have to be extra careful around Mr. Moore.

"You going to be heading up to Oliver's lumber camp anytime soon?"

"As soon as I have a full crew," Will embellished. "I was hoping some of the men might have arrived by now."

"Nope. Only people who got off were city people heading up to the Great Camps. They arrive here in their fancy clothes, thinking there will be coaches taking them. The one camp only sends down a buckboard, and it's not even covered! The men don't seem to mind the elements.

The women, they complain and squawk like a bunch of chickens in an overcrowded henhouse."

Tipping his hat back, Will studied the man. "You sure you didn't see anyone who might not have been going up to the resort?"

"Not a one." He pushed up from the chair. Standing in front of Will, he said, "Tell John his supply list will be filled by day's end tomorrow."

Just because Mr. Moore hadn't seen anyone unusual get off the last train didn't mean the person Will was looking for hadn't come into town on horseback. Though remembering the trip up from Albany, he imagined coming here by horse would be a long, tiring trip.

Will made his way down to the livery, and after asking the same questions, he discovered there had been no odd horses boarded there in recent days. He went back to the house to wait for the children and Miss Mitchell.

His stomach rumbled, reminding him he had to get the fire in the stove lit. He hoped Miss Mitchell was true to her word about cooking up a proper meal. Right now he felt as starved as a bear coming out of hibernation. The cinnamon roll had barely filled him.

Grabbing an armload of wood, he carried the cut-up logs through the back door into the kitchen. Finding some leftover kindling, he began to build up a decent fire. Once he felt certain the fire would take, he washed up at the sink and then headed into the front parlor. Standing in the doorway, he put his hands on his hips, surveying the mess. No point in procrastinating.

To start, he piled the tossed clothing back into the children's trunk, closed the latch, stood, and hefted it over his shoulder. Going upstairs, he deposited it in the first bedroom off to the left. He knew full well that this was not where Harry and Minnie wished to be; however, he needed to get a solid night's sleep. He hoped that Miss Mitchell would be able to convince them to spend the night here.

Leaving the trunk at the foot of the bed, he went back downstairs, and after setting his things right, hauled his trunk up to the bedroom across the hall from the children's.

The bed linens sat in a rumpled heap in the middle of the mattress. Will tugged and smoothed the covers as best he could. He had just tossed the pillow on top of the blankets when he heard voices and footsteps coming up the front walkway.

Closing the bedroom door behind him, Will headed downstairs to greet Harry, Minnie, and Miss Mitchell.

Will stood on the threshold, taking in the sight before him. Harry led the way, with Minnie holding on to Miss Mitchell's hand and walking at a slower pace behind him. They looked like the perfect family returning home after a day of school and work. Normalcy, something Will hadn't experienced in a very long time. He caught the smile Miss Mitchell gave the little girl, and for one brief moment he wished the look had been directed at him. Instead, when she lifted her gaze to meet his, she gave him a more cautious half smile.

She had to be feeling much as he was, wary of this new living arrangement. He'd no doubt the children would thrive under her care.

"Uncle Will! We're home!" Harry rushed past him into the house. "Miss Mitchell promised us a snack if we helped her clean up the classroom."

Will took the heavy book from her hand, saying, "I take it Harry was a great help."

"He erased all the chalk from the chalkboard and made sure all the window shades were drawn. I'd say he was a big help."

Will stepped aside to let her enter the house ahead of him. Blowing out a breath, he wondered what she was thinking of the place now that she'd be living here.

Stepping over the boy's jacket that had been tossed in a heap on the floor, she carefully took her coat off and hung it on the peg near the door.

"Harry, could you come back here?"

Poking his head out from the kitchen, Harry answered her with his mouth half-full of a sugar cookie. "What?"

"Where did you find that cookie?" Will wanted to know.

"In the basket where Miss Mitchell said they would be."

"Oh." It never occurred to him to look inside the basket. Perhaps if he'd done that earlier, he wouldn't be standing here with hunger threatening to eat away his stomach lining.

"We don't talk with our mouths full, Harry. And I need you to please come hang your coat on the hook where it belongs when you're not wearing it. And then we are going to talk about some rules that everyone will need to abide by."

Remembering all the ones she'd imparted to him yesterday, Will didn't think he could take any more of her rules. He frowned at her. Harry came into the room and stood dutifully before Miss Mitchell.

"Harry. First things first. When you come into the house, please wipe your feet and then *hang* up your coat and hat." Folding her arms, she waited while Harry picked up his coat and hat and then, standing on tiptoes, stretched his arms, attempting to reach the hook high above his head.

Taking the things from him, she said, "Your uncle can install some lower hooks for you and Minnie to use."

Will added the item to the mental list he'd been keeping.

"And Harry, I know you don't need to be reminded to wash your hands before touching any food."

Pushing his hands into his front pockets, Harry nodded.

Helping Minnie off with her coat and bonnet, she then took off her own overcoat and hung everything up. Smoothing down the front of her dress, she walked into the kitchen and began unloading the basket her father had left this morning.

"Miss Mitchell?"

"Yes, Harry."

"You said we had to wash our hands before we handled any food."

Cocking her head, she let out a little laugh. Then she reached out and rumpled his hair. "You're absolutely correct. Thank you for reminding me."

After she completed that task, she set about cooking the best meal Will had had in months, possibly even years.

A roasted chicken, compliments of her mother, mashed potatoes, and carrots graced the tabletop, along with thick slices of bread from the loaf he'd purchased at the bakeshop. As Will sat there in the glow of lamplight, finishing up the last of the meal, he was reminded of Miss Amy telling him about her friend's breakup. Watching Elsie with the children and seeing how at ease she was in the kitchen caused Will to wonder what had been wrong with the man who, according to Miss Amy, had broken Elsie's heart. And these observations didn't even take into account that the young woman was pretty. She didn't have any pockmarks, her hair was shiny, and her eyes lit up every time she looked at Harry and Minnie. A man couldn't ask for much more than that in a woman.

"Mr. Benton? Is there something wrong?"

"No. Why do you ask?"

"You've been staring at me for several minutes now. I thought maybe I had something on my face."

"No. You're fine." Embarrassed that she'd caught him, Will scraped his chair back and stood. "I'll bring in some more firewood. I need to light the fire in the parlor stove in your apartment."

"Thank you." Rising from her chair, she proceeded to clear the table.

Will left her and went to fetch the wood. On his way out to the side yard, he heard her giving soft instructions to the children. Apparently, they had some schoolwork to tend to. Once out in the fresh air, he went to the wood pile, looking up when a shadow crossed his path.

Chapter Seven

Will reached around to rest his hand on the butt of his pistol.

"Evening, Will."

Recognizing John Oliver's voice, Will relaxed. "Evening." He joined the man by the large oak tree.

"I was just out for my evening walk and wanted to see how you and the family were settling in."

Doubting that the man had simply decided to take an evening stroll, Will replied, "We're fine."

"Good. Did you learn anything at the saloon?"

"I found Lily Handland. I didn't know you were bringing her in on this assignment."

John shrugged. "She's between jobs."

"Well, she's keeping an eye on things. Promised to let me know if anyone of interest comes in." Pushing a hand through his hair, he added, "I don't need to be checked up on."

"This is a small town. Word gets out when there's a stranger about. And right now you're still considered one of those. Didn't help matters that Miss Mitchell came upon you there."

Will hoped to be able to blend in. He certainly wasn't used to other people knowing his whereabouts. It looked like he'd have a lot of adjusting to do—first having Harry and Minnie thrust upon him, then Miss Mitchell, and now being under the watchful eye of John Oliver. How was he supposed to get this job finished with so many people in the way?

"I assure you I can do this job, Agent Oliver." Will wasn't used to defending himself. It didn't sit well with him that his superior might not trust him. He knew the other agents wanted to find the bond thief just as much as he did. Will had to focus his attention. It gnawed at him that this might be the one job he wouldn't be able to see through to the end.

"Do you need anything for the house?" John asked.

"No. The house is in good condition for not having been lived in for all those months."

"I'm glad the property is suitable to you and your family." Pulling his collar up against his neck, John turned his back to the cold breeze coming down from the mountains. "I'll see you at the office tomorrow. We can discuss what I'll be needing you to do at the lumberyard."

Shivering at the chill in the air, Will said, "I'll be there first thing in the morning."

"See you tomorrow." With those words the man turned, walking off into the darkness.

Elsie dried off the last plate. She pulled the curtain aside, looking out into the dusk-filled yard, wondering what could be keeping Mr. Benton. He'd been gone a long time. She could see the woodpile and the lantern sitting on one end of it, casting shadows along the pathway. She rose up on her toes to get a better look out the window. There was no sign of him. *Where had that man gone off to?*

"Miss Mitchell, I can't decipher this problem. Can you help me?"

Setting the dish towel on the edge of the sink, Elsie joined Harry at the table.

"Let me take a look." She glanced at his crooked handwriting. Checking his numbers, she said, "Ah. Here's the problem. You forgot to carry the two. See? Now the answer is correct."

"Thanks."

The back door opened. Mr. Benton came in, carrying an armful of wood.

"I'll put this batch by the stove in your quarters."

"Thank you."

Minnie, who had been sitting across the table from her brother, yawned, reminding Elsie about the lateness of the hour. Rising from the chair, she gently squeezed Harry's shoulder.

"You finish up those last two problems while I start getting Minnie ready for bed."

It seemed Minnie had other plans. Looking up at Elsie, she gave one frantic shake of her head and then propelled herself into her brother, who was just finishing another problem. She bumped into him so hard that Harry's hand and pencil tore across the paper, ripping the sheet in half. Harry's face reddened as he let out a shout, pushing her to the floor. Minnie started to whimper. Tears rolled down her cheeks. Elsie bent down, gathering Minnie close. The little girl shook with every breath she took.

Harry shoved his schoolwork aside and said, "I didn't mean to push her, Miss Mitchell! She ruined my schoolwork." He stood at the table with his lower lip trembling and his hands fisted by his sides.

Keeping one arm around Minnie, Elsie patted him on the arm and tried her best to soothe him. "Harry, I know you didn't mean to scare your sister. But what you did was wrong. Boys don't ever push girls—or anyone, for that matter. Do you understand me?"

He nodded.

"This is a difficult time for everyone. And we all need to work together to help each other. I know it's hard for you because Minnie needs you right now. Do you think you can apologize to your sister?"

"I'm sorry I pushed you, Minnie."

Minnie wiped the tears from her eyes and then hugged her brother.

"Thank you, Harry. How about you neaten up your papers?"

While he was occupied, Elsie pondered the best way to handle Minnie's attachment to her brother. There had to be a way to give Harry the space that he needed and make Minnie feel safe. This situation wasn't healthy for either of them.

Mr. Benton appeared in the doorway. "Is everything all right in here? I thought I heard someone crying."

For the benefit of the children, she mustered up a halfhearted smile. "We're fine. Just a little mishap, that's all."

Minnie stood uncertain between them. Elsie dared to smooth a few loose strands of hair from her face. When Minnie didn't pull away, she took that as a good sign. Elsie wanted to tell her that everything would be better one day soon. She wanted Minnie to see that she could put trust in her . . . that she'd be safe and cared for. Every time she thought about what these children had suffered, she wondered anew at their daily strength.

Elsie said to Minnie, "Why don't we get your pinafore off so I can freshen it up for tomorrow?"

Minnie let her help remove the garment and watched her from a safe distance as she took it to the sink and blotted a few spots with a damp cloth. Satisfied that she'd attended to the worst of the day's wear, she draped it over the back of one of the chairs by the table.

When Minnie seemed to be fine with that, Elsie decided the best way to handle her might be to simply explain what she needed to do next. "I have a hairbrush in the next room. I can brush your hair if you'd like."

Minnie gave a slight nod, and Elsie headed into her room to take the hairbrush out of her bag. When she returned, Minnie was still standing next to her brother. Mr. Benton was leaning against the sink, watching the scene with some concern.

Elsie took out Minnie's braid and then brushed her long, curly hair. Reaching into her pocket, she took out a blue ribbon, pulled Minnie's hair back, and tied it off.

"There. Doesn't it feel better to have your hair all brushed out? This is exactly how I do mine every night."

Minnie heaved out a tired sigh.

"It's been a long day, hasn't it? Let's go on up to your bedroom." Elsie picked up on her trepidation right away. "Harry, you can come, too."

"What about my work?"

"I can tell you have a good grasp on the arithmetic. Tomorrow I'll start you on the next section. But for now, it's been a long day, so you should come along with us."

Holding out her hand to him, she caught the sidelong look he sent to his uncle. Poor Harry. One day soon she would make sure he could do things by himself without worrying about his sister. First, though, she had to make Minnie feel safe and loved.

"Do as Miss Mitchell asks, Harry," Will urged him. Looking at her, he asked, "Do you need me to help?"

"No. We'll be fine."

The children dutifully went with her up the staircase. When they made it to the second floor, the children quickly veered off to the room on the right. "No. Your room is over here." Nodding to the room on the other side of the hallway, she started to lead them there.

"We slept in here last night with Uncle Will."

"I'm sure that was special because it was your first night in a new place. But your uncle needs his own room, and he'll be right there if you need him. I'll be sleeping downstairs in my quarters. You and Minnie are lucky to have this nice room right here."

Silence filled the narrow hallway. With sagging shoulders, Harry stepped ahead of her into the bedroom. Minnie let out another tired yawn.

"I promise you if you need anything, your uncle or I will be right here." Mustering up a tired smile, she said, "Now let's get you settled for the night."

Elsie knew it would be crucial to get them used to sleeping on their own. Judging from the way Mr. Benton looked this morning, sharing a bed with the youngsters meant he'd given up a good night's sleep. Best to get everyone into a proper routine right away.

After locating their nightclothes inside the trunk at the foot of the bed, she helped them get ready for the night. Once they were tucked securely between the sheets, two woolen blankets, and a patchwork quilt, she had them say their nightly prayers.

Minnie folded her hands neatly under her chin while Harry said their prayers. "Thank you, Lord, for a good day. Thank you for bringing Miss Mitchell here to take care of us. Amen."

"That was very nice, Harry." After dropping a kiss on their foreheads, she started to blow out the bedside lamp.

"Wait! Can you keep the lamp burning? And don't shut the door."

Instead of blowing out the lamp, she turned it as low as the flame would go. Then she blew them a final good-night kiss and stepped into the dark hallway.

The tension of the long day settled against her shoulders. She knew her day had not come to an end just yet. There were still lessons to prepare for tomorrow and today's papers to grade. She waited to be sure the children had settled for the night.

When a few minutes passed with no sound other than that of the night peepers outside the house, Elsie knew it was safe to go back downstairs. Taking hold of the railing, she stepped down the first stair tread. Suddenly, light filled the lower floor.

"I thought you could use some light to find your way." Mr. Benton stood at the bottom of the staircase, holding the kitchen lantern out in front of him. He held his hand out.

Grateful for his thoughtfulness, Elsie placed her hand in his, stepping down into the parlor. "Thank you."

"Do you think they'll stay settled?" he asked, following her into the kitchen.

"I hope so. They've had a busy few days." Now that they were alone, the reality of her decision to take on this job began to sink in. Biting her lower lip, she worked at quelling the flutter of nerves in her stomach.

Her fingers still tingled from his touch. She found herself wondering what it might feel like to have his arms around her. Elsie knew she shouldn't be having such feelings, but she couldn't seem to help herself. William Benton wanted people to think him a hardened man. But she knew he wasn't. A hardened man wouldn't care about seeing to her comfort the way Mr. Benton just did. And a man like that would never let the children sleep with him when they were afraid.

When she decided to take this position, it had been with the intention of helping to care for this man's niece and nephew. She hadn't given any thought to the fact that she might have to spend time alone with him, or that being this close to him would evoke these feelings in her. Never one to have regrets, Elsie began to wonder if perhaps she had been a bit rash in making this decision.

Then her gaze fell to the pinafore drying on the chair back. Taking in a quick breath, she offered up a swift prayer for the continued strength to carry on this mission.

When she looked up, it was to find Mr. Benton watching her in much the same unsettling way he had earlier at the meal.

"What?"

"Nothing."

"Mr. Benton, you clearly have something on your mind."

Turning away from her, he offered, "Should I put the kettle on for some tea?"

Gathering up Harry's and Minnie's schoolwork, she replied, "Only if you'll join me."

"I don't drink tea."

"Thank you for remembering that I do." Thinking his kind gesture meant he was warming to her, she said, "Perhaps you could just sit here. We could talk."

"About what?"

"How our day went . . . about the children . . . about what you really expect from me." The last words came out in a whisper, and for a minute Elsie thought perhaps he hadn't heard her.

"I expect you to care for the children and this household."

"I understand that. But what about us?"

"I am the children's uncle and you are their schoolteacher. There is no *us* beyond that."

Swallowing the lump in her throat, she refused to let him see how his icy words affected her. Brushing past him, she busied her shaking hands by preparing her tea. "Shouldn't we try to be friends? I just meant to say it would be nice to talk at the end of each day. I could tell you how the children did at school, and you could talk to me about your work at the lumberyard."

Her parents always spent the end of the day doing this. Elsie took great comfort in listening to those conversations. She thought perhaps it would be nice to carry on the tradition here in this house.

When the water in the kettle had come to a full boil, she turned the burner off and lifted it from the stove, pouring the steaming water over the tea leaves. Mr. Benton might not care to have this daily conversation, but she did. Surely he cared to know how his niece and nephew were faring. She would simply tell him whether he felt like reciprocating or not.

"I think Harry is doing a fine job of adjusting to the school." Pulling the lantern closer to her, she set about getting ready to do her schoolwork. His silence seemed to take up all the space in the room. Not to be deterred, she continued her one-sided conversation.

"I'm quite sure Minnie will come along. I just wish she would speak." She took a sip of tea. Gently, she sat the cup back in its place on the delicate saucer.

"In case I've forgotten, I'd like to thank you for moving my belongings into my quarters and, of course, for bringing in the firewood and lighting my stove."

"Miss Mitchell! Do you always prattle on like this?"

The question exploded from him, causing her to jump. "There's no need to raise your voice, Mr. Benton. I'm sitting right here. I can hear you perfectly well."

"I apologize. But I told you, I don't wish to engage in this . . ." At a loss for a phrase, he waved his hand in front of his face.

"Conversation." She filled in. "We're two adults carrying on a conversation, Mr. Benton. Have you really spent so much time by yourself that you've forgotten how to carry on one?"

Casting a stern look in her direction, he replied, "I have not. I'm not used to having so many people around me, that's all, Miss Mitchell." Coming to the table, he leaned on one of the chairs. "There is one thing you could do for me."

Sitting up a bit taller, she brightened. "What is that, Mr. Benton?"

"You can stop calling me Mr. Benton. My name is Will."

Calling a man by his given name was something she'd done only once before. That man had been Virgil Jensen, and he'd led her astray with his sweet talk. The bruise on her heart was still fresh. "I'm not sure how I feel about your request, Mr. Benton."

"Tell you what, let's give this calling each other by our given names a try right now."

She stared up at him with her mouth agape. "I can't just call you by your first name. It isn't proper."

"Elsie."

Her heartbeat picked up. The way her name sounded coming from his deep, rich voice. Elsie squirmed in her chair. "Mr. Benton—"

"Will." He interrupted her. "Call me Will, Elsie." His mouth quirked up into a grin.

"Will." She spoke his name and then quickly added, "We will only do this here, when we are in this house. In public I will call you Mr. Benton and you will address me as Miss Mitchell."

His smile broadened. "Fair enough." And then he turned and left the room.

Elsie sat there alone, the shadows cast from the lamplight dancing around her the only thing left in the room to keep her company. The papers beneath her fingertips reminded her that she'd more work to do before this day was finished. Yet she couldn't concentrate.

He'd asked her to call him Will, like they were close companions. She knew that was far from the truth. Tonight one more barrier had come down. Sighing, she bent forward and focused on the task before her.

Chapter Eight

Will lay awake in his bed long before the sun rose, thinking about how smoothly the remainder of the week had gone. Elsie seemed to have a firm grip on the needs of the children, which gave him the time he needed to settle into this assignment. Miss Elsie Mitchell was an interesting woman. She was educated and gentle with the children, yet he sensed her reluctance to fully let her guard down. She was a smart woman with boundless energy. Yesterday, Saturday, he'd returned to the house after working all day at the lumberyard to find all the sheets and blankets hung up on lines stretched between just about every tree in the backyard.

True to her word, Elsie had laundered the bed linens. Together they'd brought them into the house. Elsie had shooed him outside to play with the children while she made up all the beds.

Will lay in his bed, which to him smelled like sunshine, feeling as if he were being swallowed whole. Most of his adult life he'd spent alone. Now every day he awoke to find Elsie there to greet him in the kitchen with a morning meal and fresh-brewed coffee. Since he was gone before

Harry and Minnie arose, they were always waiting for him on the front porch after he finished his day.

Unaccustomed to being needed, Will didn't know what to make of this turn in his life. He didn't want to be encumbered by a family. That's why he had agreed to hire Elsie in the first place. But he should have known that the children, with loss so fresh in their lives, in their hearts would be looking for affection from him. He was the only family they had now. Getting out of bed, he dressed and then stopped by the open door across the hall to check on Harry and Minnie.

The sight that greeted him almost brought him to his knees. Minnie lay with her back against Harry's, her doll Hazel safely nestled inside her arms. Her golden hair had come loose from the ribbon Elsie tied it with every night. Tendrils of curls lay across her delicate cheek. Harry lay with his chin resting on his hands. Their faces looked so innocent and serene.

Will knew he had to bring the bond thief to justice so they could all get on with their lives . . . wherever the road ahead would take them. He'd never imagined himself a family man. His only worry had been for himself and taking on the next assignment.

Though now, seeing these children and realizing the part they played in his life, and looking forward to seeing them at the end of each day, Will thought that perhaps his future could be different from what he'd intended.

Today was Sunday, and that meant only one thing. Elsie was going to expect him to accompany her to church. Will hoped he'd made himself clear when he told her he wouldn't be promising anything. Today was the busiest day for the saloon. He fully intended to be there to learn more about the whereabouts of the bond thief. Elsie and the children could go to the service without him.

Turning away from the children's bedroom, he walked down the stairs into the kitchen. Soft sunlight spilled in through the windows, covering the day with hope. He noticed right away that Elsie hadn't been to the kitchen yet.

He stoked the cook stove and then lit a match under the front burner. Taking the coffee percolator to the sink, he filled it with water and then added a few scoops of coffee grounds to the hopper. Replacing the lid, he set the pot on the burner. While he waited for the water to percolate, Will decided he could start the porridge. He measured the oats and water into a pot on the back of the stove. Then he took down four bowls and added them to the table setting along with spoons.

He looked up at the sound of Elsie's apartment door creaking open. The sunlight slanted across the room, landing on her. Her long dark hair hung down her back in a single braid. Still in her nightclothes, she looked startled to see him. Tightening the sash around her waist, she smoothed down the front of her dark-colored wrapper.

"I didn't expect to find you here," she said in a sleepy voice, her gaze darting to the stove where the porridge had just started to bubble over.

Without thinking, he grabbed the pot handle, then yelped as pain shot through his hand. He dropped the pot into the sink. The hot, thick liquid spilled down the side toward the drain.

Elsie flew across the room.

"Oh dear! Are you injured, Will?"

Her soft, curvy body brushed against his as she reached around him to grab a towel off the rack above the sink. Giving the water handle a few swift pumps, she ran the towel under the cold water.

Then, pressing the cold cloth against his hand, she scolded, "You shouldn't have troubled yourself with preparing the morning meal. That's part of my job."

Pulling his hand out of hers, he said, "I wanted to help you out."

Her gaze softened.

"I didn't mean to yell at you. You scared me. I thought you'd been seriously injured."

Peeling the cold compress away, he assessed the damage. His palm was the color of a beet. Thankfully, it didn't look as if his fingers had gotten burned. He didn't think there would be any blisters, but he gave Elsie the towel to drench in the icy-cold well water once more. Taking the wrung-out cloth from her, he used his free hand to tighten it around the wound. How would she have reacted if she'd known about all the serious injuries he'd suffered because of his job?

He flexed his fingers, testing out the severity of the burn. Feeling nothing more than a stinging, he said, "Let me clean up this mess and start the porridge again."

Folding her arms, she stared at him. "Absolutely not! You sit yourself down at the table. I'll get your coffee, which I see is also bubbling onto the stove. And then I'll take care of breakfast. Dear me, Mr. Benton . . ."

"Will," he said, reminding her of their agreement. Turning around as the coffee hissed and steamed onto the stovetop, he saw another mess of his doing.

"Will. You really need to leave these chores to me."

Sinking into the chair at the head of the table, he couldn't agree with her more. He watched as she moved confidently around the kitchen, preparing another batch of porridge, to which she added dried apples and a pinch of cinnamon. Now, why hadn't he thought of that? She sat a cup of hot coffee in front of him. He took a sip and thanked her.

Taking his coffeepot from the burner, she set her kettle of tea water in its place. He could get used to this. But he knew better than to think past today. No one knew what the future held. He could end up closing out the current case he was working on in a few weeks' time. When that happened, he would need to decide what he was going to do. This was the first time Will had ever doubted his dedication to the Pinkertons.

Then again, this case could take months to settle out. The children would have made a home here. It wasn't going to be long before Harry brought some of his schoolmates home to play. And Minnie . . . Will didn't think the child could take much more upheaval in her life.

It wasn't easy for him to admit, but for the first time in his entire life he finally had a place he considered a home. Elsie and the children were working their way into his carefully orchestrated life.

"Penny for your thoughts." Elsie spoke with her back to him as she stirred the porridge.

"Not for sale." Will hadn't meant the words to come out sounding gruff, but apparently they did because Elsie turned to look over her shoulder at him. He didn't quite meet her eyes. Instead, he turned to stare out the window, where another seemingly peaceful Adirondack day continued to unfold.

"I wonder what the reverend will preach about today. I've missed his Sunday services. While I was visiting my aunt and uncle, they took me to one of the big cathedrals in Albany. I must say I like our little church much better."

Will didn't know how to respond to her conversation, so he remained silent.

"You do have church clothes, don't you?" she asked.

"Elsie." He used a warning tone. "I know you've got your sights set on my attending services with you."

She fisted her hands at her hips. "You agreed to my terms of employment, Mr. Benton."

"You agreed to call me Will," he countered.

"Not when I'm angry with you." Her cheeks pinkened.

He worked at ignoring how pretty she looked when she got angry. "I told you if time allowed, I would go. I've a busy day ahead of me. John needs me to look into an altercation that took place at one of the lumber camps up in the north woods. As a matter of fact, I should be leaving soon if I'm going to be back home before dark."

Her toe started tapping and Will knew trouble was brewing.

"You won't be setting a good example for the children."

"I'll be teaching them responsibility."

"Not the right kind of responsibility."

"My providing for them is setting a good example, Elsie. I don't need you to tell me that I'm wrong to do so."

Silence descended. Elsie turned the heat down on the porridge and then left the room. She closed her apartment door behind her with such force that the pans hanging along the wall rattled. He heard something fall to the floor and then the sound of Elsie's voice. Though he couldn't make out what she said, he could only guess her anger was directed at him. Will didn't know what to make of her actions.

Rising from the chair, he went to her door and knocked. "Elsie?"

She didn't answer, although he thought he heard the sound of a drawer being closed. Trying again, he called out a bit louder. "Elsie, please open your door."

"Is there something wrong with Miss Mitchell, Uncle Will?"

The sound of Harry's voice startled him. He said to Harry, "She's fine. Just upset with something I said is all." He was surprised to see them dressed in their Sunday best. Even Minnie's doll Hazel wore a different outfit. And now that he took a closer look, he saw that the pretty blue-flowered dress was a perfect match to the one Minnie wore.

"It's church day, Uncle Will. Miss Mitchell laid our clothes out for us last night before we went to bed. You aren't wearing that, are you?" Harry pointed at Will's worn work pants and flannel shirt.

"What's wrong with what I've got on?"

"Ma always said you should put your best self forward when going to church. And you're wearing your work clothes."

He hadn't thought about his sister in a long time. He couldn't remember the last time he'd shared a meal with her. Maybe it had been that time at Christmas when he'd been passing through between assignments. That would make it at least five years ago. The twins had been toddlers. Will doubted they would remember.

"You're right, Harry." Pain filled his heart as he thought about the loss of his sister. "Your mama would scold me if she could see me now."

"She said you always squirmed during church services."

He frowned at the memory. He had indeed squirmed his way through many a church service, mainly because he'd thought it was cruel and inhuman to expect a child to sit through an hour and a half of listening to Preacher Bailey go on about the Good Book. *That man could quote chapter and verse. Seemed like he never found much of the good in the Good Book to preach about, though.* Perhaps that was another reason Will had strayed from the church.

He ladled the hot porridge into the bowls and set one in front of each of the twins. Then he added a splash of milk from the pitcher and a drizzle of honey out of the small pot Elsie kept on the window sill.

Harry stuck the spoon into his bowl and slurped a big mouthful of the oatmeal. He said, "You better get dressed, Uncle Will, or you'll make us late."

"What have I told you about talking with your mouth full, Harry?" Elsie said, walking into the kitchen wearing her Sunday dress. The fabric was the color of springtime buttercups. She'd taken her hair out of the braid and wore it lose. The curls spilled softly over her shoulders, down to the middle of her back.

His own breakfast forgotten, Will stared at her, thinking how lovely she looked. She avoided looking at him, busying herself by wiping Minnie's mouth. Then she sat down at the opposite side of the table. Taking the cloth napkin from the place setting, she took great pains to smooth the fabric just so over her lap.

"Harry and Minnie, you did a fine job of getting ready for church. I'm very proud of you." Still avoiding Will's gaze, she asked, "Did you remember to say grace?"

Harry looked toward him for guidance. Will sighed, rolling his shoulders. It seemed he couldn't do anything right today. "We didn't get that far," he answered for Harry.

"Are you going to be joining us, Mr. Benton?"

Pulling out his chair, he sat back down and folded his hands in front of his bowl while Elsie recited grace. Afterward, he listened while Harry chattered with Elsie about the approaching church service. She promised him they could stay for lemonade and cookies if he and Minnie behaved themselves during the service. This news made his nephew very happy.

Swinging his attention back to him, Harry urged, "Uncle Will, you best be hurrying to get ready!"

He lifted his gaze to look across the table at Elsie. Slowly, the reason she'd been upset with his earlier choice not to attend church began to sink in. He needed to set a good example for these children. He needed to do right by his sister. Certainly, he could give them an hour of his time. Besides which, the informant he wanted to meet with would be at the appointed place all day.

Clearing his throat, he replied, "Just give me a minute to change into something more appropriate."

Feeling quite pleased with this turn of events, Elsie pushed away from the table. She cleared the dirty dishes and filled the sink with water, washing and setting them in the dish rack to dry. The day turned brighter as sunlight filled the nooks and crannies of the house. She made her way into the foyer, gathering their coats off the hooks.

She called out to the children. "Harry and Minnie, come put your coats on! The air is still cool."

Harry kept trying to squirm out of her reach.

"Goodness, Harry. Stand still."

"I need to get outside."

"We'll be out there in a minute." After buttoning him up to under his chin, she turned to help Minnie. "You look so pretty this morning."

Elsie wasn't certain, but she thought she saw Minnie's mouth curl upward just a tiny bit. "Go join your brother on the porch."

Minnie moved past her. Elsie stood. Her breath caught in her throat at the sight of Will as he came down the staircase. He'd brushed his dark chestnut hair back off his forehead, and a few stubborn locks curled against his white shirt collar. Dark pants and a black vest with a string tie completed his church attire. He wore a smug expression, like he knew just how appealing he looked. Truth be told, she thought he looked perfect—except for the gun belt hanging from his hip.

She knew she'd be pushing her luck if she asked him to leave the gun behind. Even so, the question worked its way out of her mouth before she could stop it. "Can't you leave your weapon here?" She knew the men all wore those guns, but still you'd think on the Lord's Day they could leave them at home.

Reaching around her, he took his hat from the rack. Then, leaning so close she could see the golden specks in his brown eyes, he said, "I've made all the compromises I'm going to for today. Don't push your luck, Miss Elsie." Winking at her, he settled his hat on his head.

Grabbing her gloves from her coat pocket, Elsie pulled them over her fingers and went out to join the children. Will pulled the door closed behind them. They walked side by side to the main road, looking for all the world like a normal family. But she knew it would be dangerous to start to think they were any sort of family.

All around them birds were singing and newly formed sprigs of green grass poked through the sun-soaked soil. Up in the distance she could see her neighbors and friends gathering in front of the simple, whitewashed clapboard church. The single spire rose up from the roofline to meet the robin's-egg-blue sky.

Her best friend Amy stood on the bottom step talking to Elsie's parents. She saw Elsie and waved. Elsie waved back. Hurrying along, she met up with them. Slightly out of breath, she bid everyone a good morning. Her mother pulled her into an embrace. "Elsie! I've missed you."

"Oh, Mama, I've missed you, too. Remember I'm only a short wagon ride away. Papa can bring you into town anytime for a visit."

"I know. We should plan for regular Sunday dinners."

"I'd like that. And I think it would be good for the children."

The church bell rang, signaling the service was about to begin. They filed in, entering the third row from the back on the right-hand side of the sanctuary. This was the same pew Elsie's family had sat in for as long as she could remember. Taking his hat off, Will sat on the outside of the pew. The minute he settled, he began to fidget.

He fussed with his burned hand, opening and closing it. He adjusted the hem of his coat. He set his hat on one knee, then picked it up again moments later to hang it on the hook under the hymnal stand. Picking up one of the hymnals, he thumbed through the pages. At first Elsie thought he might be looking for something in particular, but the way he kept flipping the pages told her he was still fidgeting.

She tapped him on the shoulder and gave a slight shake of her head, hoping he would understand he should stop acting like a schoolboy. Pulling his mouth in a firm line, he placed the hymnal back in the stand. Which, of course, was a silly thing to do because the Reverend Finley came to the pulpit instructing the congregation to open to page fourteen to sing the opening hymn, "My Lord, What a Morning," one of Elsie's favorites. Collectively they rose to their feet for the singing. Afterward, Reverend Finley led the congregation in the opening prayer. He closed with amen, and everyone sat.

No sooner had Will settled than Harry started squirming. Wiggling back and forth like a caterpillar, he bumped into first Elsie and then Minnie.

"Harry. Sit still," Elsie whispered.

His body stilled. In the next instant his hand shot out. Plucking a hymnal from its stand, he proceeded to mimic Will's earlier actions.

Except Harry's fingers crinkled every page he touched, causing several of the parishioners to give Elsie chastising looks. Taking the book from him, she picked him up and sat him on her lap. Wrapping her arms about him in a loose hug, she stilled him against her.

Today's sermon concentrated on opening one's heart to those in need. It spoke of forgiveness and tolerance for those less fortunate. Elsie listened as the reverend quoted from the scripture, Mark 11:25.

"And when you stand praying, if you hold anything against anyone, forgive him so that your Father in heaven may forgive you your sins."

The words made Elsie think about Virgil. Though his betrayal had hurt her deeply, she was working at finding it in her heart to give him full forgiveness.

"I beseech each and every one of you to look around you, to find those who have wronged you, and to forgive them. Because only then will you find the power to live your life freely. Only then can you open your hearts to help those in need. Heartston is a small but loving community. We are so blessed to have people who are willing to open their arms, to offer comfort and support for the less fortunate."

She glanced at Will out of the corner of her eye to see if he was listening. He sat tall against the seat back. His eyes were narrowed in concentration. She wondered what he was thinking about. Could there be someone in his life he needed to forgive?

She felt uplifted by the sermon, as if the words were meant for her and this small family she now lived with. Minnie's head rested against her side, and Harry had finally quieted in her arms. With Will by their side, she found herself wishing for more. Elsie took some comfort in knowing that for now having Harry and Minnie to care for would have to suffice.

The sermon ended and the congregation sang the closing hymn. They walked out into the brilliant sunshine. Harry tugged at her skirt.

"Miss Mitchell, we behaved, didn't we?"

With the exception of all the fussing and fidgeting he'd done, she thought they had behaved.

Looking down at Harry and Minnie, she answered, "Yes. You and your sister can go join the other children for refreshments."

But Minnie didn't go with him. Instead, she stayed by Elsie's side. Elsie shielded her eyes from the sun as she watched Harry run off to the backyard, where a long table had been assembled and filled with homemade cookies and pitchers of fresh lemonade. Harry jostled his way into the line of children. Elsie looked at Minnie, who stood with Hazel in one arm and seemed a bit bereft without her brother near her.

"Would you like a cookie and drink, Minnie?" Elsie asked, gently taking hold of her free hand.

Minnie shook her head.

"All right then, we'll wait here for your brother."

Will came up beside them. "Nice service."

Elsie smiled up at him. "Thank you for accompanying us."

"All part of our agreement, Elsie."

"We agreed to address each other properly when in public, Mr. Benton."

"You're correct, Miss Mitchell. I forgot."

She looked around to make sure no one had heard him address her in such familiar terms. It wouldn't do for any more rumors to be started about their arrangement.

John Oliver approached them. Tipping his hat, he said, "Good day, Elsie and Will."

"Hello, Mr. Oliver. Isn't it a fine spring day?"

"Indeed. I hate to interrupt, but I need to speak to Will."

Elsie watched the two men saunter off to the edge of the church-yard. They bent their heads together, speaking in hushed tones. *What could that be about?* It seemed she wouldn't have to wait long to find out because Will was making his way toward her.

"I have to go to work."

"On the Lord's Day?"

"It can't be put off any longer, Miss Mitchell. I believe I told you this morning that I had work to attend to on behalf of the Oliver Lumber Company. Besides which, I just held up my end of the church part of our bargain."

"Yes, you did." Peering up at him, she added, "I sincerely hope you came away with some good thoughts from the service."

He grinned. "What I came away with is the thought that not a lot has changed about sitting through a preacher man's long-winded sermon since I was boy."

Elsie just felt thankful that he'd joined them at all. "Will you be home in time for supper?"

"I'm not sure how long this will take."

Hiding her disappointment, she said, "We'll see you later, then."

Tipping his hat to her, Will set out in the direction of the Oliver Lumber Company office. As soon as he was out of sight of Elsie, he veered to the right down an alleyway. Moving into the shadows of a row of stacked, empty shipping crates, he kept close to the outside wall of the saloon, looking for a back entrance. Finding it situated between some beer kegs and yesterday's trash, he opened the door and entered a dark hallway. He passed by a closed door through which the sounds of muffled female laughter could be heard, followed by the deep rumblings of a male voice.

Will pulled his long duster coat closer, hiding his sidearm. A smoky haze filled the barroom. He could smell stale beer and whatever the day's meat special was. Empty peanut shells crunched under the heels of his boots as he made his way to the last vacant spot at the long pine bar. Looking at the reflections in the dingy mirror, he studied the raucous crowd of lumberjacks and saloon girls. Three bearded men were lined up at the opposite end of the bar, doing shots of whiskey.

A pair of saloon girls sidled up to them. He caught the eye of the redheaded one. Lily came up to him and wrapped her arm around his waist.

"Hey, stranger. You want to dance?"

Will bit back a laugh. Lily was certainly getting into her role. "Not today."

"How about you buy me a drink instead?"

"All right." He ordered two beers.

Picking up a mug, Lily tapped the rim of his. "Cheers!"

Will continued to scan the room. Where was the thief hiding? When would he trip up and leave them a clue?

"He isn't here." Lily commented.

"I know." He wrapped his hand around the mug. Rolling his shoulders back, he tried to relieve some of the knots at the base of his neck.

Keeping up their ruse, Lily pressed her body against his. "You seem to be on edge, Will."

"I'm fine, Lily."

"I think you're a bit off your game."

His gaze hardened. "I'm *fine*."

She backed away from him. "All right."

He took hold of her hand, pulling her back. "I'm sorry."

"We need to work together, Will. There's an abandoned farm a few miles north of town. Go out there and take a look around."

She pushed the beer mug away from her. The bartender came over.

"I think you got a customer looking for a dance partner." He nodded in the direction of a short bald man who stumbled toward them.

Lily looked at Will, rolled her eyes, and then let the man sweep her off onto the dance floor.

Laying a coin down on the bar next to the untouched beer, Will paid his bill and left. He stood at the edge of the walkway, waiting for two wagons to pass. He walked through the wake of their dust to the stables. Once there, he hired a mount and left town.

Will headed in the direction Lily had indicated, up the hillside that curved along the back edge of the village. The innocent sound of children's laughter faded away behind him as he and the horse climbed toward the base of one of the mountains.

The horse picked its way through small patches of lingering snow. A cold draft surrounded them as the sun darted behind a cloud. Will burrowed into his duster, wishing he had on his heavier shearling coat instead. He nudged his knee against the horse's flank, urging the mount to the left. There wasn't enough daylight left to explore farther up the mountain.

Up ahead he spotted a flock of sparrows diving and darting along the path of the spring winds. The horse tugged against the bit, and Will loosened his hold on the reins, letting the horse wander to the south. Here the earth gave way from rocky outcroppings to hard-packed, half-frozen muddy pathways. Will turned the horse downwind, following what looked to be an old cattle path.

They came to a group of farm buildings surrounded by an over-grown pasture and a crumbling split-rail fence. He could see a two-story house. Some of the siding had fallen off, and boards covered the broken windows flanking the front door. The shutters on one of the windows dangled in the breeze, held on by a single surviving hinge. The place looked abandoned.

The base of Will's neck tingled. He rubbed the spot. Pulling the reins in, he brought the horse up short. The mare pawed lightly at the ground. Dipping her head to the earth, she found a few sprigs of new spring grass to munch on.

Will sat up tall in the saddle and took in the deserted house and barn. This had to be the place Lily had told him about. Dismounting, he led the horse along while he checked around. He came across more pieces of fallen siding, a broken wagon wheel, and what looked to be the remains of a woodshed. He knelt beside a set of animal tracks. Rubbing his hand over the indentations, he thought they could be from a deer. He'd seen small herds of them out in the back fields on the outskirts of town.

Standing, he looked toward the old homestead. The nape of his neck itched. Will couldn't find anything out of the ordinary here. And yet his senses were telling him something different. The horse looked at him as if to ask, "Are we done here?"

Leading the horse out into the open, Will walked up an overgrown pathway that stopped at the remains of a front porch. An old hitching post listed to one side near the bottom step. Will looped the reins around the post and left the horse. A thick forsythia bush hid half of the bottom step. Will picked his way around it. Climbing along the edge of a rickety board, he stepped up onto the porch.

He jiggled the handle on the front door, surprised when it gave way. Pushing the door halfway open, he looked through the shaft of light into what used to be a hallway. Dust motes floated through the musty air. He caught the scent of old decay. Off to his right stood a staircase covered in cobwebs. Wandering over to the base of it, he noticed that none of the webs had been disturbed. Their wispy tendrils wove unbroken over the steps connecting to the newel post.

Turning away from there, he walked along the opposite wall until he found a doorway. Looking inside what appeared to be some sort of a sitting room, he saw an old ladder-back chair. The caned seat had long ago been worn through. From the light slanting through the boarded-up windows, he could see a thick layer of dust covering the floorboards. A trail of mouse tracks meandered around the walls of the room.

Satisfied there were no signs of human life here, he poked his head into two more rooms. At the back of the house he found a room with a low, slanted ceiling. A rusty cook stove took up half of one wall. Next to that was a door that he assumed led to the backyard. But that was not what caught and held his attention. Moving to the stove, he knelt on the hard-packed dirt floor to inspect a lopsided stack of wood. The pieces of wood weren't logs at all. They were sticks and twig branches that looked as if they might have been collected from the surrounding woods.

There wasn't a cobweb or speck of dust on them. He put his hand on the front of the stove. It was ice cold to his touch. He ran his fingers over the dirt floor, trying to find any sign that someone had been here recently. It was hard to discern whether the indents he felt were from a boot or just another sign of the aging property. Standing up, he went out the back door. Slowly he walked around the outside of the house, coming full circle back to the hitching post.

The mare nickered, pawing her front hoof along the ground.

Will patted her side. "I know you're ready to get moving. I've got one more thing to check on."

He repeated his earlier movements around the perimeter of the barn. Here and there he knelt down for a closer look at the patterns in the hard earth. Shaking his head, he finally came back around to the front of the barn, satisfied that no one had been here in a while. Maybe the wood pile in the house had been gathered by a vagrant.

He gave one last look around, thinking that maybe whoever had been here had moved on a long time ago. Even if that were the case, Will decided he would come back out here in a few days to check on things. Going back to the mare, he released her from the hitching post and swung up into the saddle, turning the horse toward town.

From the back of the barn, Virgil waited for the man to ride off the property. A trickle of sweat dripped off his forehead. Stepping out from behind the stack of hay bales, he crept to the front of the barn. Pulling back one of the doors, he stepped outside. That man had come out of the hills. Virgil didn't know who he was. But one thing was for certain: the way he looked around, kneeling to check the tracks on the ground—snooping inside the house—he moved like a lawman.

Stepping out into the shadows, Virgil walked to the house—the house where he'd been born and raised by his God-fearing parents, gone nigh on five years now.

Careful not to make any new tracks, he stepped inside the footprints the man had left behind. He entered the back door. His gaze fell on the wood he'd collected earlier. Now that the man had been poking about, Virgil couldn't risk having a fire in the cook stove.

Reaching into his pants pocket, he pulled out a hunk of the hardtack. He sat cross-legged on the floor with his back up against the wall. Sticking the shoe leather–like substance between his teeth, he tore into it like a starved animal.

He stuck his tongue out, running it along the edge of his lip, feeling the ridge of the cut he had gotten last week. The night he'd been in a fight in the Albany alleyway was still fresh in his mind. It's why he'd come back to the Adirondacks. Time was running out.

He'd been evicted from the prestigious Saint Anthony Hotel on State Street three weeks back for failure to pay his bill.

His instincts, what remained of them, had told him to keep his newfound secret stash hidden away. So he'd left the hotel, finding refuge in a hideous excuse for a rooming house, the stash secured. He wasn't proud of the way he'd come by these reserves. A few months back he had stumbled upon a drunken hobo in a railroad boxcar he was traveling in. The fool had bandied about the fact that he'd come upon some stolen railroad bonds. Virgil had waited for the man to pass out and then fleeced him of the bonds. They were precious pieces of paper, and he refused to use them to pay for something as unworthy as simple room and board. He wanted to keep them for a bigger game. Except when he'd found and played the bigger game, he hadn't been prepared.

Because he'd heard the rumblings and rumors about how those bonds were being hunted down by lawmen and bounty hunters alike,

Virgil knew he had to hide them until there came a time to either sell them to another disreputable person or use them in a card game. He'd become aware that the Pinkerton Detective Agency had been hired to locate the bonds and knew time was of the essence. And then, in what he could only call divine providence, he'd run into his former fiancée, Elsie Mitchell.

Elsie may have still harbored resentment toward him for the way he'd jilted her, but she also had a weakness to forgive those less fortunate. His trust in that sent him to her the very next day, asking her to take the envelope where he'd carefully sealed the bonds.

If anyone had been following him over the past decade, they could have foreseen his downfall. From the time he'd been a young lad pitching coins in the school yard, Virgil had loved the feel of taking a chance. No matter what the stakes, what the cost, you could count him in the game.

Years ago when his mother had learned of his sins, she'd quoted from the Bible. "No servant can serve two masters. Either he will hate the one and love the other, or he will be devoted to the one and despise the other. You cannot serve both God and money."

Virgil had chosen the latter.

Staring into the fading daylight, he started planning his next move. He didn't know whether Elsie had discovered what she'd been keeping for him. What if she knew and decided to give the bonds to the authorities? What if his creditors were closing in? His head started to ache. He shivered. Laying himself on the floor, he curled up, trying to find any warmth he could. He looked at the cold stove, wishing he could have a fire. He closed his eyes and thought about getting the bonds back.

The walls were closing in on him. He shivered again, drifting off.

Chapter Nine

Elsie rolled over in her bed, blinking remnants of sleep from her eyes. Underneath the edges of the drawn curtains, the soft pink glow of dawn seeped into the bedroom. Snuggling deeper beneath her quilt, Elsie wiggled her toes, wondering what had awakened her at this hour on a Saturday. The one day of the week when she didn't have to be up at the crack of dawn, and here she was wide awake. Her nose twitched. She smelled coffee. Pushing the covers aside, she sat on the edge of the bed. She heard the sounds of footsteps moving about the kitchen. Then came the distinct sound of the motion of the sink pump handle. A steady stream of water splashed against the bottom of the sink.

Poking her feet under the bed, she located her slippers. Sticking her feet in them, she stood up, took her robe off the bed post, put it on, and quickly made her way to the door. Cinching the belt securely around her waist, she slowly opened the door and peered out.

"Will! You're home!" Surprise and relief flooded through her. Stepping into the kitchen, she noticed his pants were covered in dried mud. He stood in stocking feet. She could only imagine that he'd left a pair of equally muddy boots outside.

He turned around. "Elsie! Good morning. I'm sorry I woke you. I was trying to be quiet."

The room was shadowed in the early light of day. Elsie quickly made her way to the table. Taking the globe off a lantern, she lit the wick. "Are you hungry? I could make you some eggs and bacon."

She bustled about the room, gathering up two place settings. "The children collected the eggs from my mother's henhouse. My father has offered up a portion of his flock to us. We were out there for dinner this past Sunday. They love the farm; it's so different from living here in town. You should have seen Minnie running after those hens! I think she could be starting to trust others a bit more."

"Elsie?"

She stopped moving and looked across the room at him. "Yes, Will."

"You're rambling."

"I'm sorry. You've been gone so long, and there's so much to catch you up on." She went to the stove to start the kettle for her tea. "The children have missed you something fierce."

She picked up her teacup and saucer, bringing the set to the table. Turning around, she watched Will wash his hands and then splash water on his face. Joining him at the sink, she grabbed a towel from the rack and handed it to him. Their fingers touched. Beside her, Will stilled. He gathered her hands inside his and gently gave them a squeeze. He looked as if he had something important to tell her. Instead, he released his hold and she dropped her hands to her side.

Wiping his face and hands dry, he hung the towel up, turning to face her again. "I'm sorry about the children."

Elsie studied his face, noticing right away the week's growth of beard covering his strong jawline. Fine lines fanned out along the edges of his dark eyes. He looked tired.

"They've been through so much over the past few months. They need continuity. They need to see you more than once or twice a week." Softening her voice, she added, "They think of you as a parent, Will."

Will's face paled. For a fleeting moment Elsie saw something in his eyes. Panic or fear? She couldn't tell. *"Will,"* she raised her voice. "You had to have known they were beginning to feel this way."

He pushed away from the sink and walked over to the stove. Taking one of the tin cups from the shelf, he poured the coffee into it. His shoulders moved up and down as he took in and released a deep breath.

"I'm doing the best I can."

Elsie knew he was working hard to make a better life for Harry and Minnie. Still, they needed more than food on the table and a roof over their heads. They deserved to feel as loved as they did when their parents were alive.

She shook her head at him. "I don't understand how you can keep holding them at arm's length."

"I'm trying, Elsie. Isn't that enough?"

She bit her lower lip in frustration. She knew he meant well, but sometimes, especially where children were involved, a person had to make a firm commitment to doing the right thing. She would give him a little more time to see how things ought to be. Eventually, William Benton would need to figure out where Harry and Minnie fit in his life.

He took his place at the head of the table. "I'm here right now."

"For how long?"

He took a sip of coffee and replied, "I don't have to go back up to the camp for a few days."

That wasn't the answer she'd hoped for. But if that was all he could commit to right now, then it would have to do. "Minnie and Harry will be happy to find you here when they wake up."

They didn't have to wait long for the children to join them. Harry came downstairs first. Entering the kitchen, he rushed to Will's side.

"Uncle Will! You're home! You're home," he chanted, running in circles behind Will's chair. "I prayed last night that you would come home! And here you are."

Elsie laughed. "Harry, you're making us dizzy with all of your running around."

Will surprised her by grabbing Harry up in a bear hug. She hoped this meant he could see their need. Snuggling his nose alongside Harry's neck, Will said, "I missed you, too, Harry." Harry leaned against him, smiling like he'd just gotten the best gift a boy could ask for.

"Harry, sit down next to your uncle. Is your sister awake?"

He shook his head. "I think she's still sleeping."

"I'm going to go check on her."

Before Elsie could move, she caught Will tilting his head in the direction of the stairs. Elsie walked over to find Minnie standing on the last step.

"Well, good morning, Minnie." Elsie reached for her hand. Minnie slid hers into Elsie's. They walked into the kitchen. Elsie said, "Your uncle Will is home."

Minnie let go of her hand and walked over to Will. She stopped just short of where he sat. She cast a lopsided smile up at him and then sat in her chair. Elsie dared to meet Will's gaze. His face softened. Elsie hoped he felt the same way she did. Happy and content. These children brought light into their lives . . . into his life. Will wouldn't always have her as his buffer between the children. He needed to let them into his heart.

Tying on an apron, Elsie set about making breakfast. While the bacon sizzled in a pan on the back burner, Elsie broke half a dozen eggs into a bowl. Picking up a wooden spoon, she broke the yolks. Stirring the eggs together, she said, "I have a meeting with the Lord's Acre Picnic committee today. Perhaps, Harry and Minnie, you'd like to stay here with your uncle while I'm gone."

"I think that's a good idea," Will said.

Elsie had half expected him to say no. "Are you sure?"

"Yup."

"Then it's settled." Dishing the eggs and bacon onto plates, she set them on the table.

"What's this Lord's Acre Picnic?"

She brightened at his interest. "The picnic is an annual event, held the last Sunday in June. Everyone in the town comes. After our worship service, we gather outside for a large potluck. There's everything from turkey to apple dumplings. We set all the food out on long tables. There are games for the children. And someone always starts up with a bit of music. I've never missed one."

"Sounds like a good time to me."

"I'm glad you think so, because we'll need plenty of help setting up. I'll be sure and put your name on that list."

"Elsie," he said in a warning tone. "You know I can't plan that far ahead."

Ignoring him, she ate her breakfast. After they finished, Elsie accepted Will's offer to clear the table. She washed up and changed, and realizing time was getting on, she rushed to help Minnie and Harry get dressed. Coming back downstairs, she joined Will on the front porch.

"The meeting should take only a few hours."

"Don't worry."

She frowned, even though she knew they would be all right without her. "I'm not worried. I think you'll be fine."

Will stepped in front of her. Brushing his finger lightly down her nose, he said, "Oh, you're worried. I can tell because you're crinkling up your nose."

"I don't crinkle my nose." She brushed aside his hand.

Will let out a laugh, shrugged his shoulders, and said, "If you say so."

Harry skipped down the front walkway with Minnie trotting along behind him. Elsie started to call out to the children to not go beyond the gate when she heard a commotion on the street.

"Clear out of the way!" A man shouted. "There's a runaway horse!"

Elsie and Will both ran back, but Minnie had already stepped out into the road. The horse charged toward her.

"Minnie!" Elsie screamed. Harry started after his sister, but grabbing his arm, Elsie pulled him to the side of the road. He struggled against her, trying to break free so he could go save his sister. Elsie held on to him for dear life.

Will pushed past them, running through the gate and into the road. He reached out and snatched Minnie right up off her feet, holding her fast against his chest. The beast galloped past, coming within inches of them, its hide covered in sweat and foam frothing at its mouth.

A man from the livery ran past them, shouting and waving his arms above his head. He called for the horse to stop. Eventually, another man ran out into the roadway, caught hold of one of the reins, and pulled the horse to a halt.

By now a few of the shopkeepers and some townsfolk had stopped to see what all the commotion was about. The man who'd been chasing the horse came over to them.

"I'm so sorry. The horse broke free while I was trying to get a stone out of one of his shoes." Looking at Minnie and Harry, he asked, "Are the children all right?"

Minnie squirmed against him. Will just held on tighter. Not ready to let her go.

"We're all okay." His voice came out sounding gravelly. He swallowed down his emotions. "You'd best get that stallion back to the livery."

The man apologized again and then headed off. Over the top of Minnie's head, Will caught sight of Elsie and Harry. In two quick strides he went to them. Without thinking, with his free arm he pulled Elsie to his side. She leaned into him.

"You're trembling," he said.

"I was so frightened!" Her voice came out in a whisper.

"Me, too." Looking down at her, Will saw his fear reflected in the depths of her violet eyes. Never in his wildest thoughts could he have imagined the feeling of fear that tore through him when he'd seen that horse bearing down on Minnie. It was as if time had stood still, and for one horrible moment he thought this sweet little girl would be taken from them. He knew Elsie didn't think he had strong feelings for these children, but he did. The close call had proved one thing: Will would do anything for Harry and Minnie.

Elsie blinked up at him. "Thank you."

Pulling her closer, he whispered, "You're welcome."

The heat of her body seeped through her cloak, warming him. Will's heartbeat quickened. Between them the children squirmed.

Elsie rested a hand on Minnie's back as if to reassure herself one more time that the child would be fine. She took a small step back, moving out of Will's embrace.

Minnie still had her arms wrapped firmly around his neck. She surprised him when she plunked a wet kiss on his cheek. Gently, he set her on the ground. Squatting down to her eye level, he said, "You are one brave little girl."

Minnie nodded.

He ran his hands over her shoulders and arms just to be sure she was really unharmed. Satisfied, he stood up. He watched Minnie go off to join her brother in the front yard. Then he looked at Elsie, who had been watching him the whole time. His hands shook. He shoved them in his pants pockets and gave her a crooked smile.

He asked, "Are you all right?"

She put a hand over her heart. "I think I had the life scared right out of me."

"I know what you mean."

"I'm glad. Because now I know one thing for certain."

"And what's that?" he asked, even though he knew exactly what she was going to say.

"You can't deny your feelings for your niece and nephew."

Turning, he rested his elbows on the gate, watching Harry and Minnie play on the walkway. He had never denied he had feelings, but until now he'd had no idea how deeply they ran. Keeping his back to the schoolteacher, he said, "I would have done that for any child."

"William Benton, why are you being so stubborn?"

The wind kicked up again, sending a flurry of old dried leaves into the air. He wouldn't take her bait, not today. Not after what had just happened.

And yes, he could be as stubborn as the day was long. Just to prove it, he asked, "Don't you have a meeting you need to be getting to?"

He heard her huff.

"If you are quite certain that you will be all right, then I will take my leave."

"We'll be fine. And don't worry, I won't let them play anywhere near this roadway."

"I know you will keep them safe."

Thinking he'd been too hard on her, Will looked over his shoulder at her, set on telling her to have a good meeting, but she'd already walked out of hearing distance.

Will left the twins sitting on the top porch step to go into the house. Now that he had time to look around, he noticed how the house had changed. It looked like a home. Elsie had hung curtains in the front windows and rearranged the furniture. Two chairs and a round table sat in front of the fireplace. She'd moved the small settee to the other side of the room, nestling it under the front windows.

He made his way toward the kitchen and then stopped dead in his tracks. There hanging on the wall, just to the right side of the coat rack, were a pair of stunning black-on-white silhouettes that had not been there before. Running his finger over the edge of the frames, he recognized the images of Harry and Minnie. Down in the right-hand corner of each picture were the initials E. M. He wondered when Elsie had found the time to do these. He imagined she'd had little time to herself this past week.

He'd been out at the lumber camp, helping John with the work crews. Up until a few short months ago, Will hadn't any idea of how busy a lumber camp could be. Since the melting snow had filled the creeks with water, the loggers were floating their wintertime harvest downstream to the mill in Heartston. As the weather warmed, the activity would switch to processing the logs into lumber. He envied his friend. Even though John had been a devoted Pinkerton agent, he'd managed to come back to his hometown and build a successful business.

Will had no idea what he would be doing if he hadn't found his life's calling with the agency. He certainly didn't think he'd find himself living in a small mountain town with two small children to look after.

"Uncle Will! Are you coming back outside?" Harry called from the front porch.

Will hurried to the front door and answered, "Yup. I'm right here."

"Miss Mitchell took us out to her old house. We had a nice dinner with her parents, and we got to gather the eggs from the henhouse. Her ma said we could keep the ones we gathered, and then Miss Mitchell's pa drove us back into town. He left those plants over there so we could plant our very own garden." Harry nodded to a spot on the far side of the walkway.

Craning his neck around, Harry peered up at Will, adding, "Poor Miss Mitchell's been so busy we haven't had any time to get those plants in the ground. Just look at them, Uncle Will. They're getting all droopy."

Standing on the top porch step, Will could see where the plants had been left in the front yard, sitting out in the bright sunlight. Even though there had been a few dewy mornings this past week, it hadn't been enough to properly water the plants. He went over to take a closer look at the plantings to see if they could be saved.

Harry and Minnie joined him. Will put his hands in his pockets while he decided if they could be salvaged. Out of the corner of his eye he caught Harry mimicking his moves. The boy stood right next to the fence post, his hands stuck in his front pockets, peering down at the cuttings.

"What do you think?"

All in all they didn't look too weakened. "I think we should find a proper spot in the side yard to plant a garden."

Harry lit up like a nighttime lightning bug. Jumping up and down, he chanted, "We're going to grow a garden! We're going to grow a garden!"

Will laughed. Minnie stood quietly by his side with that lopsided grin on her face. "Minnie, would you like to help us plant the vegetable garden?"

She nodded.

"I think between the three of us we can get these to the side yard in one trip. What do you think, Harry?"

"Yep!"

Because she wouldn't set her doll down, Will gave Minnie the smallest tomato plant. She cradled it in her arms right next to Hazel, following him and Harry out to the yard.

"Let's put these on the back step while I find the best place for the garden." Will walked around the yard with Harry and Minnie at his heels every step of the way. Finally, he settled on a patch of soil right outside the kitchen-sink window. This would be perfect. By his calculations the summer sun would come around here in the midafternoon, giving the plants ample sunlight. Elsie would be able to see the garden growing from the kitchen.

Going to the small shed in the backyard, he found an old shovel and a hoe with a half-broken handle. These would have to do. When he returned, he found Minnie sitting on the step by the back door, playing with her doll, and Harry poking at a tiny hole in the ground.

"You all ready to get to work?"

"Yup! Can I use the shovel?"

"No. I'll dig up a few rows and then you can help put the plants in." He and the boy worked side by side, with him digging and Harry picking up the large stones they unearthed.

"How's school going?" Will asked. "You been behaving for Miss Mitchell?" He asked the question even though he knew Harry to be a good student.

Picking up one of the rocks Will had cleared from the soil, Harry tossed it onto the growing pile. "I'm always good, Uncle Will. Though the boy whose father runs the post office, Avery Scott Jr., he's been having a hard time with his arithmetic. Miss Mitchell has been giving him extra help after school."

"That's good of her."

"Yeah, I guess." He shrugged. "I like it better when we can come straight home when school lets out."

"She has a job to do."

"I know. How's your job been going?"

Will rested his hands on top of the shovel handle. "I've been busy working up at the lumber camp." He despised himself for having to tell the half-truth to this innocent child.

"That's good. You've been gone a lot."

"Working long hours is part of what I have to do, Harry."

"I know. It's just . . ."

"Just what?"

"We miss you when you're gone. Miss Mitchell, she does a lot of work at school, and then when she comes home, there's work for her to do here."

"I see." Will wasn't sure how he could explain his absence to Harry in a way that would make the boy feel any better. So he said, "Let's get this garden planted, and then that will be one less thing Miss Mitchell has to worry about."

For the next hour they worked the soil, turning the rich dirt and making rows. Then, while Harry handed him the plants, Will dug holes, and together they put the plants in the ground, covering their roots with the dark soil. Straightening up, they stepped back and took a look at the results of their labor.

"Not too bad for a few hours' work." Will planted his hands on his hips, observing their little garden.

"Soon we'll have tomatoes for our dinner!" Harry grinned up at him.

"It takes a few months for them to grow and mature. But I'd say if the weather cooperates, we'll be enjoying ripe tomatoes by the end of summertime." He put the gardening tools back in the shed and then rejoined the children at the back stoop.

Hugging her doll close, Minnie pointed at Will. He wished she would speak to him. *What would it take to get her to do so?* He might not know a whole hill of beans about raising children, but his instinct told him to be patient a bit longer.

"Something bothering you, Miss Minnie?"

He waited as Harry went over to her and she whispered in his ear, pointing again at Will.

"She thinks you need to wash up before Miss Mitchell gets home."

"Does she now?"

Harry nodded.

"Well then, I guess I'd best get a move on." They followed him into the kitchen. He said, "Harry, your hands are covered in dirt. I'll help you get washed up first."

Lifting the pump handle up and down, Will waited for the fresh water to flow into the sink. Then he helped Harry wash his face and hands. Minnie held out her hands, and he took a cloth from the edge of the sink, wet it, and then gently rubbed it over her hands.

Afterward, he put a stopper in the drain and filled the sink partway. Then he took his straight-edged razor from the windowsill, soaped up his face, shaved off the past week's beard, and then cleaned up the sink. When he finished, he went upstairs and changed into fresh clothing.

Finding the children on the front porch, he said, "Let's set the table for dinner."

As he gathered the plates and silverware, Harry asked, "Do you know how to cook, Uncle Will?"

"I can manage some eggs and campfire grub."

"Maybe one day you and me, we could go camping, and you could show me how to cook like that."

Will couldn't make a promise. He didn't want to think beyond what tomorrow might bring. He still had to find the bond thief, and once the job finished up, he didn't know where the next assignment would take him. Looking from Harry to Minnie, he knew leaving them wasn't going to be easy.

It was nigh on time he set about coming up with a plan.

There was a possibility that his sister Mary Beth and her husband would return from their European trip and want the children back. Considering the way she'd left them, Will didn't think it the best solution, but it would keep them out of an orphanage. His heart ached at the thought of placing them there or with his sister. After what had happened earlier with Minnie, Will knew he would fight to give them a good home.

"Uncle Will?" Harry's voice brought him out of his thoughts.

"Are you going to cook our supper? We had eggs for breakfast. Is there something else you can cook?"

"Let's see what's in the pantry." He went to the small anteroom off the kitchen. Minnie and Harry trailed after him.

Minnie picked up a can and handed it to Will. Beans. He could handle opening a can and heating the contents. Harry found a loaf of bread. Will spotted a platter covered with a cloth. Lifting the cloth, he found a portion of a leftover roast. This would definitely do. He picked up the platter. On the way out of the pantry he spotted a jar of applesauce.

"Harry, grab that jar for me."

The boy stood on tiptoes and gathered the jar between his hands. "Miss Mitchell is going to be happy when she sees what we're cooking up."

Will hoped so. After he set everything to heating on the stove, he followed the children back outside.

There, Minnie led them to a patch of spring violets. He let her do the picking, and when she handed him the small bouquet, smiling up at him like a cherub, he knew his life was changing. The light- and dark-purple hues of the flowers reminded him of the color in Elsie's eyes.

Back in the house he found an empty canning jar, filled it partway with water, and stuck the flowers inside. He put the arrangement in the center of the table. The floorboard creaked, and he turned around to find Elsie standing in the doorway, looking as lovely as those spring violets.

"The table and *you* look wonderful."

Rubbing his hand over his clean-shaven chin, he grinned. "Harry and Minnie made me clean up and they helped with the table."

Wandering over to the stove, Elsie lifted the lid on the pot and peered in at the simmering beans. Will had left the roast on the counter, figuring they could eat it at room temperature. He'd found a bowl to dump the applesauce in.

Elsie spun around. "You all did a fine job."

Harry and Minnie came to stand on either side of her. "Wait till you see the surprise we have for you!" Harry beamed up at her.

"You're preparing our dinner is surprise enough."

Tugging at her hand, he said, "Come on outside!"

They went out the back door and around to the side of the house. "Uncle Will and I planted a vegetable garden."

"Oh my!" Tears sprang to her eyes. "This is quite the surprise. Thank you!" Pulling Harry close to her side, she hugged him and then dropped a kiss on Minnie's head. Finally, her gaze settled on Will. "You didn't have to do all of this for me."

"Harry said you've been too busy to get the plants in. We had the time." He didn't want her to make too much out of the project. He'd been happy to finally be able to help out around the house.

"It's lovely."

"Uncle Will says we'll have vegetables to eat by summertime."

"Indeed."

They went inside for their dinner. An hour later, with the meal finished and the dishes washed, dried, and put away, Elsie found herself sitting on the top porch step next to Will. He had gone to a lot of trouble to plant the garden and set the table. This past week had been a long one for her, and she hadn't realized how tired she was. Will's thoughtful gesture had revitalized her. What pleased her even more was that he had come home and spent time with the twins. Harry and Minnie were chasing a butterfly around the front yard.

She looked up at the sky. The sun had begun dipping low on the far horizon. The warmth of the day lingered in the air. She said to Will, "It is a beautiful evening. The best one yet." Deep inside, she knew it was the best one yet because he was here with her.

"Elsie, I'm sorry I haven't been home more."

"I knew what I'd be getting into when I agreed to take the job, Will. I understand you have work to do and you can't always be here."

"Still, Harry tells me you've been staying after your class lets out to help the postmaster's son with his schoolwork. And then you come back here and you tend to the children. It can't be easy."

"Nothing worth doing in life comes easy, Will."

"True enough. What made you decide to become a teacher?"

She couldn't keep the joy from her voice. "I've always loved learning about new things. I love being with the children. It seemed like a natural fit. When the former schoolteacher retired, the committee asked me if I wanted to take the job."

She brushed an ant from the toe of her shoe. "Nothing gives me more pleasure than when I see the faces of my students light up because they understand something I've been teaching them."

"What about a family of your own? Do you think that is in your future?"

Her heart skipped a beat. She shook her head. She wanted to tell him that Harry and Minnie were filling that void in her life. "Right now my days are filled with so many joyous things."

They were silent for a few minutes until Will asked, "You know what our front porch needs?"

She shook her head.

"Rocking chairs. So we don't have to hurt our backs sitting on these porch steps." Resting his hand against his lower back, he added, "I'll see if the mercantile has any. If not, I'll have someone at the lumberyard make us up a pair."

"I'd like that." What she would like even better would be if this moment could last forever. Will actually wore a look of contentment on his face. And he'd spoken the words "our front porch"—as though he'd begun to think of this as their home.

After the sun began to set, Elsie called the children into the house to get ready for bed. She sat on the edge of their bed listening to Harry recite their bedtime prayers.

"Thank you, Lord, for bringing Uncle Will home and for keeping us safe. Please watch over Miss Mitchell. Amen."

Turning down the lantern, she left them. There could be no denying her growing attachment to the children. With each passing day, they became a bigger part of her life. Elsie had to find a way to stay detached. She needed to keep reminding herself that she was their caregiver, that they didn't belong to her. It was becoming more and more difficult to remember that.

Going to her apartment, she found the travel book where she'd left it the last time she'd looked through the pages. She'd been hoping to plan some geography lessons using some of the places highlighted in the chapters. Then some of the students had needed extra help, so between seeing to their needs and caring for the twins, her free time had been limited.

Tonight she needed to take her mind off Will's family. She needed to remind herself why she'd taken on this extra job to begin with. She needed to start planning her next trip. One day Will might decide he no longer needed a live-in caregiver. Or he could find a woman to make his wife, and she would become the mother figure for Harry and Minnie. Each beat of Elsie's heart made her ache at those thoughts.

Wiping the tears from her cheeks, she picked up *The Smithson Travel Guide,* thinking it would be best if she concentrated on what lay between the pages. A light tapping on her door made her turn around.

Chapter Ten

"Elsie?"

Setting the book on the side table, she stood, smoothing down the front of her dress, and walked over to answer the door. She pulled it open. "Is there something else you need me to do, Will?"

"No. I'm reheating the last of the coffee and thought you might like me to put the kettle on for some tea. Would you like a cup?"

"I was going to work on some lesson plans." She nodded toward the book.

"Is that the travel book you received last month?"

"Yes. I haven't had time to look through it, and since the children are snuggled in bed, I thought I might get to it tonight."

Part of her wanted him to leave so she could get on with her project, and yet a bigger part of her hoped he would persuade her to join him for the tea.

Then he surprised her by saying, "Bring the book out into the parlor. I've a fire going. You can sit by the hearth. I won't bother you while you work, Elsie."

"All right. I'll have one sugar cube for my tea, please. Oh, and there are some tea biscuits in the round tin on the shelf over the stove."

"I'll find them."

Making her way into the parlor, Elsie couldn't help but think how cozy the house was looking. She'd rearranged the furniture. Her mother had come by and measured the windows, then had surprised her with the airy muslin curtains that were hanging there now. She'd worked on the silhouettes of Harry and Minnie while Will had been up at the lumber camp. She'd wanted to surprise him with a keepsake of the children.

He entered the room carrying a tin tray lined with two mugs and a plate filled with the tea cookies. She waited until he'd set the tray on the end table and then said, "Thank you."

"You're welcome."

Elsie opened the travel guide on her lap. Surprisingly enough, the first page she opened to had a journal entry from a young woman who'd traveled on a steamer ship to Europe with her parents. The trip of Elsie's dreams. Just reading the young lady's account had her thinking of what she'd pack in her trunk for such a journey.

Will rested an elbow on the arm of his chair, then took a peek at the book. "Europe. Never been. Seems to me it'd be a long trip."

Even though Will had said he wouldn't interrupt her, Elsie didn't mind talking about her plans. "The sailing time could be anywhere from seven to ten days, depending on the weather. If the ship hit high seas or storms, it could be longer. But think of all the interesting people I could meet on a ship. There would be plenty of time during the transatlantic crossing to learn about their lives and what made them want to travel to such faraway places."

He scrubbed his hand along his chin. "I don't know, Elsie, seems to me if you do this, you should go with a traveling companion." The side of his mouth tilted upward, and there was a gleam in his eyes as he said, "A woman as pretty as you, I dare say there'd be men toppling over each other to get your attention."

She blushed and turned away from him, pretending to rearrange her skirts. "I'm used to traveling alone."

"This wouldn't be a trip that is just along the Hudson River. You'd be going thousands of miles."

"I suppose I might be able to find someone to go with me."

"Maybe your friend Amy could go."

The idea that Amy would have the money needed for such a trip made Elsie realize that reaching her dream might be further away than she hoped. Disappointment surged through her. "I can tell you think this trip is nothing more than my fanciful daydream."

"Why would you say something like that?"

"Because, Will, I am on a meager schoolteacher's salary, and Amy is barely making ends meet."

"It's nice to have dreams, Elsie."

What Will didn't understand was that Elsie would find a way to make this dream come true. She flipped to the next page in the book. Here was a depiction of the interior of one of the luxury liners that were now sailing out of New York City. She ran her fingers over the picture. Maybe she would have her students come up with ideas on where they could travel and how they might get there.

She felt Will's hand on her arm.

"Elsie, I didn't mean to upset you. I'm sorry."

"No. You were right. I'd never thought about needing a traveling companion. And, of course, I know how expensive the trip will be." Trying to brighten the mood, she said, "My students will enjoy the geography project I'm planning."

He removed his hand from her arm and leaned back in the chair. "I like sitting here in front of the fire. I noticed you added some things to the house while I was gone."

"I hope that's all right. It seemed the house needed some warm touches."

"I want to thank you for those portraits you did of Harry and Minnie, too."

"You're welcome. They're called silhouettes." She laughed remembering how she'd had to entice Harry to sit still. "Minnie sat perfectly still while I drew her likeness, but Harry, he squirmed like he had ants in his pants! I finally promised him one less arithmetic problem for homework if he sat still long enough for me to finish."

"I'm glad everyone is settling in."

"Children thrive when their life has routine." She absently turned another page. "Will, they appreciated the time you spent with them today."

"I had a day off."

"I know, but surely it brought you closer to them."

He didn't respond. Elsie wondered what he was thinking. Was he remembering the day he'd shared with the twins? Was he happy enough here to eventually make this a permanent home? Will interrupted her thoughts.

"How did your meeting go?"

"We got a lot accomplished."

Elsie stared off into the fire, watching the flames curl around a small log, shooting sparks up the chimney. Elaine Moore had wasted little time rushing to tell her how her husband, Francis, had seen Will coming out of the saloon earlier this week. Though she'd tried, Elsie couldn't understand his need to go there. She wondered if he had a gambling problem. Maybe he liked to imbibe, or heaven forbid, he spent the time carousing with those women.

She didn't want to imagine any of those possibilities. Something kept drawing him there. She knew asking him might make him angry, but she was willing to risk ending this peaceful interlude.

Elsie shifted in her chair, turning to face him. The soft glow of firelight filled the room. Will's eyes were closed. His mouth relaxed. Elsie nibbled on her lower lip. Finally she spoke. "Will?"

"Hmm?"

"I need to ask you something and I want you to promise me you won't become angry."

He opened his eyes. Her heart stuttered as she stared into his gaze. His pupils darkened. Elsie watched as he raised his eyebrows. She could feel the shift in his demeanor. Maybe she'd been wrong to ask him to make any promises.

"I'm listening."

Suddenly she didn't feel so brave. Before the nerves got the best of her, Elsie said, "Elaine Moore joined us at the committee meeting today. Do you know who she is?"

"Francis Moore's wife." Will repositioned himself in the chair.

"She told me her husband has witnessed you leaving the saloon." The words came out in a rush. A log in the fireplace rolled backward, sending more sparks up the chimney.

Leaving her chair, Elsie found the long-handled poker and pushed the log back into place. Behind her, Will remained quiet. Determined to find out why he was patronizing the saloon, she turned to face him.

"I seem to have forgotten that Mr. Moore knows everything that goes on in Heartston," he said.

"He is a bit of a gossip," Elsie agreed. She rested the iron poker alongside the fireplace wall. "I don't understand why you are going there, Will." She turned to face him again.

"We discussed this issue before."

"I know. I thought that since you seem to have settled here, you weren't frequenting the establishment anymore." Of course, she'd no idea where he'd really gone when he wasn't home. This past week had shown what Will had said from the beginning—that he'd be gone long hours and maybe for days at a time. But to think he would rather spend his free time in the saloon than be here with the children got Elsie riled.

Deciding to take a more gentle approach, she pushed back her ire and chose her next words carefully. "Perhaps you shouldn't be going there when you are needed at home."

"Are you preaching to me, Elsie?"

She straightened her shoulders, staring him down. "I'm not! I'm just trying to point out that your time could be better spent."

Will left the chair. Striding across the room, he stopped in front of the window. He yanked back the curtains. She watched him flex his shoulders. The growing tension between them sliced through the air like the cold blade of a knife.

"Why do you go there?"

"It's not for the reason you're fearing."

She couldn't voice the worst of her fears. Memories of her encounter with the redheaded saloon girl gave way to goose bumps rising. Elsie rubbed her arms. She should be praying for that young woman's salvation, and instead she harbored feelings of anger and frustration at Will.

"Elsie, you need to trust me when I tell you I have my reasons for going there."

She joined him by the window. "What reason could be more important than being with Harry and Minnie?" she asked, pushing him to give her answers.

She saw him closing his feelings away. Shutting her eyes, she said a short prayer, asking the Lord for strength. Opening them again, she found Will still staring off, but this time there was an anguish she'd never seen before in him.

Softly, she continued, "Will. Please. Talk to me."

Knowing he couldn't open himself to Elsie's questions, and yet realizing he had to give her something, frustrated Will. How had his life come to this? Could he tell her some of what she wanted to hear and not risk revealing who and what he really was?

Will didn't know, but he owed it to Elsie to at least try.

Keeping in mind that his first loyalty was to the Pinkertons, he avoided meeting her gaze, staring out into the inky night.

This wasn't at all how Will had planned for his life to be turning out. He knew full well the children were beginning to see him as their father figure. And what of Elsie? She cared for them like a mother. Heaven above, he needed to close this case. He needed to decide what would be best for the children. And while he'd been busy tracking the bond thief, the children and the schoolteacher had been busy building a home—his home.

"Harry and Minnie love living here, Will. And I know one day soon Minnie will speak to us. But we both need to be here; we both need to be in their lives."

He spun around. "This is all temporary! One day you'll have saved the money you need for your big trip and then you'll be gone. You're no different than I am. Why can't you see that, Elsie?"

She brushed her hand across her eyes, and he realized she was trying to keep tears from spilling down her cheeks. Feeling like the worst sort of cad, he took her trembling hands in his.

"I'm sorry. Please forgive me. I never meant to say those words. Oh, Elsie . . ."

She squared her shoulders and said, "You may see me in the same light as yourself, Will, but I give my all to caring for your charges. When you are out at night doing whatever it is that you do, I am the one here seeing to their well-being."

"I know you are. And I am grateful you can be here for them when I'm not able."

"You'd have more time with them if you avoided the saloon."

He blew out a frustrated breath. "I'm there on business. All right. That's all you need to know."

Bowing his head, he did something he hadn't done in a long, long time. He prayed. He prayed for forgiveness and for strength. Elsie brushed her hand lightly over the top of his head. Her hand stilled. Lifting his head, he looked into her tear-stained face expecting to find anger, but instead he saw compassion and patience, neither of which he deserved.

Reaching out, he cradled her face in his hands. Her skin felt so silky smooth to his touch, reminding him of that day long ago in Albany when he'd first met her. Her skin felt as soft and inviting as those silk stockings had as they slipped through his fingertips. Except . . . he didn't want whatever was happening between them to slip away from him.

Letting out a groan of frustration, he released her, and slowly rising said, "I need to go out for some air."

"Will, please—" She followed him to the door.

"I'll be back later."

Later turned out to be hours into the night. When he finally returned to the house, he found Elsie had left a lamp burning for him on the kitchen window sill. He carried it with him to light the way up the stairs, where he looked in on the children. Then he sat wearily on the edge of his bed.

Pulling off first his coat and then his boots, he lay back against the pillows and fell into a fitful sleep.

Chapter Eleven

Elsie came out into the kitchen on Monday morning to find a low fire burning in the firebox underneath the stove, but no sign of Will. Once again she'd lain awake for hours last night until she finally heard him return. During that time her thoughts had tumbled around in her mind. The weekend had been tumultuous. There had been the frightening incident with Minnie and the runaway horse, and then coming home after the committee meeting to find the garden planted and a meal on the table.

Will and the children had been making great headway. Elsie saw how tender he'd been with them. Her thoughts swirled back to what Elaine Moore told her about Will and how he reacted when she confronted him. *What sort of business could he be conducting in the saloon of all places? Why did he always seem so reluctant to be honest with her?* She felt like even though he'd been trying to open up with her, he was holding something back. Elsie vowed she would get to the bottom of this, one way or the other.

Putting the kettle on for tea, she left the kitchen and made her way upstairs to roust the children.

The door to Will's room stood partway open. She gingerly stepped into his room. The scent of him lingered along with something else—the distinct odor of cigar smoke. Yesterday's shirt lay haphazardly over the foot of the bed. Picking it up, she brought the chambray fabric to her nose.

They say that certain scents hold memories, and for her this meant only one thing: Will had gone to the saloon last night.

"Oh, Will, what have you done?" she whispered.

"Miss Mitchell!"

Harry called out to her from across the hall. Replacing the shirt where she'd found it, Elsie went to say good morning to the twins. "Good morning, Harry. Good morning, Minnie. I hope you slept well."

Stretching his arms high above his head, Harry answered for both of them. "We did. Can we have maple syrup on our porridge?"

Mustering up a smile, she replied, "Only if you get dressed and are downstairs in the next ten minutes."

She'd been teaching them how to tell time and found giving them little games helped them understand.

"Go!" She called out the time and watched them scurrying about. Minnie came over with her pinafore undone. Elsie spun her around and buttoned up the back. Harry pulled on his socks, then raced past her to the stairs.

"Don't run, and hold on to the railing!" She called out.

Taking hold of Minnie's hand, she followed Harry into the kitchen. Checking the time, she said, "You've got a minute to spare."

Getting breakfast on the table and everyone fed and ready for school kept Elsie's mind preoccupied. But once they were walking into town, her feelings of dismay and frustration crept back in. *How had the weekend started off on such good footing only to end with hurt feelings?*

Virgil made his way into Heartston on foot in the afternoon. The hour-long walk gave him plenty of time to think. The day after that man had been snooping around his property, Virgil had fallen ill with a fever. He'd lost track of how many days went by before he felt well enough to get out of the house. He'd washed out his clothes, drying them in the sun, and then shaved off his two-month-old beard. After dressing and combing his hair, he set off.

He knew Elsie could be trusted to keep the bonds safe. Today he'd get them back and then sell them off. Maybe he'd pay his debtors and find another game to get in on. Either way, today he'd be moving on.

Since school would still be in session, he made his way to the schoolhouse first. Elsie would be surprised to see him, but he'd told her when he'd given her the package to expect him later.

Up ahead he saw the school yard, the same one he'd gone to as a young boy. Except his teacher had been old Mrs. Krumpkill. She was strict and as mean as a riled-up rattlesnake. He'd be willing to bet every last stolen bond that Elsie never, ever disciplined with the hard end of a long switch.

Pausing to stand among a grove of birch trees, he watched Elsie come outside. She rang the bell, and the children rushed out of the schoolhouse and down the steps. He heard her tell them to be careful and to walk, not run. When all but two of the children had gone, she went back inside. Virgil wondered who the youngsters were and why they remained. They went over to play on the swing.

He stepped out of the shadows, walking quickly across the school yard. He took the steps two at a time. When he entered the schoolhouse, he found Elsie with her back to the door. He watched as she cleaned off the chalkboard.

"Elsie."

She spun around, dropping the eraser on the floor. "Virgil! What on earth are you doing here?"

"Elsie, I'm sorry if I frightened you." He came toward her with his hat in hand.

She smiled at him, though he could see the wariness in her eyes. "You didn't frighten me. I didn't hear you come in."

She was lying. She was nervous. He could tell by the way she kept looking out the window to see the children. And then her gaze would dart back to him, but she couldn't quite bring herself to meet his gaze.

"Is there something I can do for you?"

"Do you remember that package I gave to you back in Albany?"

"Yes. I still have the envelope."

"Do you think you could get it for me?"

"Right now?"

"As soon as possible. Please, Elsie, I need to get it back."

"I left it at my parents' house when I moved into town."

"You moved into town? Where are you living?"

"I'm over at John Oliver's grandmother's place. It's complicated. I'm helping out a friend."

Again she didn't look at him fully. She knotted her hands together. Versed in people's tells, he wondered why she was lying to him.

"I'm not going back to my parents' house until next week. Can you wait until then?"

Tiny beads of sweat broke out along his brow. He needed those bonds straightaway.

"Do you suppose I could go out there myself and ask them to get my things?"

"Virgil, my parents don't know where I put the envelope."

When he didn't move, she added, "I promise I'll get it for you as soon as possible."

He didn't want to pressure her. She might begin to suspect his true motives. "I guess I can wait till then."

"You should come to church. I'm sure there are plenty of your old neighbors who would like to see you again."

136

"I doubt that, Elsie. I imagine there are a lot of them who still want a piece of my hide over what I did to you."

A flicker of pain crossed her face.

"Time has a way of allowing forgiveness," she spoke softly.

"I understand and appreciate your forgiveness, Elsie."

"It hasn't come easily for me. But I've moved on."

"I know you have."

From outside, there came a shout.

"I'm afraid I have to go check on the children."

In a rustle of skirts, she rushed by him and out the door. Going to the window, he saw her kneeling next to a young boy. She was rolling up his pant leg, then checking his knee. Even from this distance he could tell she was being gentle with her touch. Then she kissed what had to be a sore spot from a spill the boy had taken off the swing.

Turning away from the window, Virgil left the schoolhouse, trusting Elsie would get him what was rightfully his.

By the time Elsie had made sure Harry's injury wasn't serious and gone back inside to gather her things, Virgil had left. *What a strange visit.* He looked a mite better than the last time she'd seen him back in Albany, but something still appeared to be amiss with the man.

She'd been so busy this past month that she'd completely forgotten about the envelope he'd given her to bring back here. She wondered what was so important that he had to have it back—he'd seemed upset that she couldn't lay her hands on it right away. Locking the door behind her, she joined Harry and Minnie at the bottom of the steps.

"Harry, I'll get you a cold compress for your knee once we're home."

"It's feeling better. Just a scrape is all."

On their walk home, Minnie picked some wildflowers to add to the bouquet they kept in the middle of the kitchen table. The new ritual had begun the day Will had set the violets there. Elsie thought it a lovely gesture, one which brought Minnie great pleasure.

"Miss Mitchell!" Harry called out. "Look what's on the porch!"

Elsie looked up to see two white slat-board rocking chairs sitting in the middle of the porch, aligned so whoever sat there could have a full view of the front yard.

"Oh my. Aren't they lovely?"

"They sure are."

Will had made the comment about wanting some rockers, and lo and behold, here they were. She followed the children up the steps. Walking over to the first rocker, she couldn't resist the temptation to sit down, testing it out. She pushed her toes lightly against the porch floorboards, setting the chair in a gentle rocking motion.

Will had been correct, sitting here sure beat sitting on the porch step at the end of a long day. Relaxing into the chair, she took a moment to give thanks for the day. Minnie climbed up onto the other rocker and leaned her body forward and back, matching her rocker's beat to Elsie's.

"This is nice, isn't it?"

Minnie nodded.

"We'll have to be sure to thank your uncle Will." Noticing the flowers Minnie had picked lying by the front door, Elsie reluctantly rose and picked them up. "It's time to get these in some water."

Minnie stayed on the porch. Harry quickly occupied the spot Elsie so recently vacated. Seeing them so happy in the chairs made her think perhaps Will could hang two swings in the yard for them to play on. Once in the kitchen, she set the flowers down beside the sink. Going to the table, she took the canning jar from the center and picked out the wilted flowers, changed the water, and put the new ones in.

She put the freshened arrangement back in the center of the table. Then she pulled the curtain on the window aside and peered out to check on the children. They were still sitting contentedly in those chairs. Harry was chatting away to Minnie, who occasionally leaned toward him. With every new dawn, Elsie hoped it would bring them closer to Minnie's healing. She longed to hear the sound of the child's voice.

As soon as she had dinner cooking on the stove, she called the children in to wash up and help get the table set.

"I've been thinking perhaps your uncle could hang up some swings for you children to play on. What do you think of that idea?"

"I like it a lot, Miss Mitchell," Harry said from where he stood at the sink washing his hands.

"Harry, I've been thinking. What if I let you call me Miss Elsie while we're here at home. Would you like that?"

"I would, Miss Elsie!" He beamed at her.

"And when you're ready, Minnie, you may address me in the same manner."

Minnie wrapped her arms around Elsie, hugging her middle. Reaching down, Elsie stroked the top of Minnie's head. Every day, more and more, the girl was opening up.

"Oh dear, Harry. I almost forgot about the cold compress for your knee." Releasing Minnie, she took a cloth from the sideboard. But Harry stopped her.

"Don't worry, Miss Elsie. I'm feeling a lot better now."

"I'm glad to hear that. Dinner will be on the table shortly."

While they sat down, Elsie puttered about putting the finishing touches on the meal. As the day drew to a close and the dinner hour was upon them, she wondered if Will might be joining them. She hadn't seen hide nor hair of the man since their conversation the other night. Elsie knew the cooling-off period would do them both some good. Still, she found she missed him.

She'd just filled their three plates with slices of venison, boiled potatoes, and some pickled beans when she heard the front door open and close. Will's place was set, ready for him when he came home.

Harry's eyes lit up. "Uncle Will's home!"

"I am." He entered the room, heading straight to the sink to wash up.

When he was seated, Will helped himself to the meat and vegetables, saying, "I trust everyone had a good day."

Harry said, "Miss Mitchell had a man come to visit her, and I fell off the swing in the school yard. But I'm all right, just a little scrape on my knee. I can show you." Harry started to lift his pant leg.

Elsie stopped him by saying, "Harry, it isn't polite to show our wounds at the dinner table."

"Sorry." Putting his pant leg down, he returned to finishing his meal.

Elsie felt Will's gaze upon her. No doubt he was wondering who her visitor had been. She'd never spoken of her relationship with Virgil. Frankly, she didn't think it any of his business. She'd put Virgil out of her life a long time ago.

When the rest of the meal was finished up, she saw to the cleaning of the kitchen. Will had gone upstairs. She turned her attention to homework and getting the twins into bed.

When she finally had time to return to her remaining tasks, the sun was hanging low on the horizon. She heard the creak of the rocking chair. She looked out to find Will sitting on the porch.

"Come join me."

Since she'd been tiptoeing around the creaking floorboards in an effort to not disturb the sleeping children, Elsie was amazed he'd heard her. She swore the man had the hearing of an owl. Opening the front door, she stepped out into the sweet night air. She took a moment to savor the peaceful moment, then moved past Will to take the remaining seat. The night peepers began their chirping. Off in the distance a wagon rattled along the roadway toward town. A soft breeze caught in a wisp of her hair. She pushed the strand off her forehead.

Will asked, "You had a gentleman caller at the school?"

"I did."

"Anyone I might know?"

"He's an old friend. Someone from my past." Now why had she gone and added that? Will would want to know more. She had closed the door on that painful and embarrassing experience.

"Elsie?"

"Hmm?"

"Is this man someone special?"

Would it bother him if Virgil were still special? Because even if Will did not want to admit to it, there had been a definite shift in their relationship.

She remembered how she had pushed him to talk about his past. It seemed only fair that she tell him about hers. She said, "We were going to be married."

His chair stilled, then started rocking again.

"You sure don't mince words."

"You didn't expect my past to include a man. Is that it, Will?"

"Don't put words in my mouth. I already knew you were once engaged to be married."

"Who told you?"

"Your friend Amy."

"Why would she do that?"

"She wasn't passing along gossip, if that's what you're thinking. I believe she told me as a warning for me to treat you kindly. So, this man who came to see you, was he your former fiancé?"

"Yes. His name is Virgil Jensen."

"If he bothers you for any reason, I want you to let me know."

"Will, I doubt he will do me any harm. He came by to ask me to return something to him."

"Now what could you possibly have that belongs to him?"

"It's a package he gave to me when he saw me in Albany. I'll give it back to him the next time I see him, and then he'll be gone. You've nothing to worry about, Will."

His hand shot out to cover hers, stilling her chair. "Elsie Mitchell, of course I worry about you! You're a loving and caring woman—the prettiest schoolteacher I've ever seen—and I don't want to see anyone hurt you."

With those words, he got up and walked off the porch.

Elsie sat in stunned silence. If she ever doubted for one moment that Will had growing feelings for her, this just confirmed it. But what did it mean for the two of them?

Chapter Twelve

Will made his way over to the lumberyard, hoping he'd find John Oliver still in the office. Most days the man remained at his desk, working long into the night. He saw the lantern light spilling out the window into the alleyway outside the office. Tapping lightly on the door, he called out, "John, you in here?"

"I'm in the back."

Stepping around crates of nails, Will walked through the narrow doorway into his boss's inner sanctum. John barely looked up from his hunched-over position.

"What can I do for you, Will?"

"I need to know about Virgil Jensen."

Those words caught his attention. John looked up at him through narrowed eyes. "Why?"

Will took a seat in the chair facing the desk. "He stopped by the schoolhouse to see Elsie today."

John gave Will his full attention. "May I ask what Elsie told you about him?"

Even though Elsie had put on a brave front, Will could tell she still carried around some hurt over the man's rejection. And he didn't know the specifics of why Virgil Jensen had jilted Elsie. He thought the man had to be an idiot to leave behind someone as kind and giving as Elsie.

"She didn't tell me much, just that they were engaged. She has something that belongs to him and he wants it back."

"Any idea what that might be?"

"Just a package he gave to her when she was visiting her relatives down in Albany is all she told me. Do you remember them being together?"

"They were together for such a short time. Virgil's family had a homestead on the outskirts of town. His parents died a while back from influenza. He didn't even come back for their funeral. They're buried out in the back of the cemetery."

So Virgil hadn't had the wherewithal to come back to attend his parents' burial. Or maybe he hadn't known of their passing at the time. Either way, a man not caring enough about his family to see to a proper burial didn't sit right with him.

He rubbed his hand along the base of his neck. "This place, is it about an hour north of here?"

"Give or take. Why?"

"I may have been out there the other day. I'd gone out for a ride and came upon a run-down farm. Had a barn, couple of out buildings, and a house that has seen better days. I looked around but didn't see anything out of the ordinary." He paused and then added, "I did get a feeling while I was there."

Cut from the same cloth as Will, John would know what Will meant. Most Pinkerton's worked off their gut instincts. It was what kept them alive.

"Maybe Virgil was there."

"Is he a dangerous person?"

"I've never heard of him having any run-ins with the law. He kept to himself as far as I remember. I might have seen him going into the saloon. I heard some rumors about him being a gambler." The corner of John's mouth quirked up. "You feeling he might be encroaching on your territory?"

It took him a minute to realize that John thought Will saw Virgil as a threat to Elsie and him. "Elsie and I have an agreement that involves the children and the running of the household, nothing more."

The lie rolled off his tongue too easily. The truth was, if his life were normal and he really could settle down, he'd pursue Elsie's affections in a heartbeat.

But as hard as he tried to keep his distance from the woman, she managed to be in his thoughts more than he cared to admit.

John looked back to the paperwork on his desk. "If you say so."

Regret tugged at his insides. Will couldn't afford to be distracted by any feelings for her. "I do. So what do you think Virgil is up to?"

"I'm not sure. We'll just keep an eye out for him."

"I know he'll be coming around to see Elsie again. Maybe it's time I stayed close to town for a bit."

"Agreed. You can work over at the lumberyard for a few days. That way you can have set hours every day."

For the first time in a long while his life had taken on a routine, something he thought had slipped out of his reach. Being on the road, moving from place to place, chasing the next assignment . . . that had been his life. Now he had a place to come to every night, a hot meal on the table, two young children awaiting his return . . . and the schoolteacher.

She greeted him with a smile at the end of most days. And there were those days when she greeted him madder than a riled-up hornet's nest—mostly because he'd been absent from the dinner table or more recently because he'd missed a church service. One thing was for certain, his life had become better because of her.

And because of all that, he had more to lose.

The wind had been blowing something fierce. Elsie had started the laundry at the crack of dawn, hoping to get all the bedding washed and hung up on the line before noontime. Though it was a good day for drying, she'd been struggling with the gusts for a better part of an hour now. The last of the sheets slapped against her side, leaving wet marks on her skirt.

Slinging the sheet over the line, she managed to clip the clothespin snugly over the end of the linen just before another gust came barreling through the yard, picking up the empty wicker basket and tossing it about.

With the wind whipping her skirts about her ankles, Elsie stumbled through the yard, chasing after the basket. She finally caught up with it, trapped between a pair of men's black boots. She straightened up to see Virgil standing there.

Virgil saw the look of apprehension in her eyes. He hadn't meant to startle her. Quietly, he said, "Good thing I came along when I did, Elsie, or you would have been chasing that basket all over town. The wind is kicking up mighty fierce today." He held the basket in his hands.

Her hair had come loose from the ponytail she'd tied it off in. Elsie batted the strands away, at the same time tugging the basket out of his grasp.

"Virgil! What brings you here on this blustery day?"

"I need to talk to you. I thought since it being a Saturday and all that you wouldn't be tied up with the schoolchildren."

She took a small step away from him. He saw movement behind her. Two sets of little feet poked out from underneath the sheets drying on the line.

"You got some company?"

"I'm helping a friend care for his niece and nephew."

"I see," he said, even though he didn't.

The children giggled. "Must be hard on you teaching all day and then having to come here to take care of children that don't even belong to you."

"Virgil! You shush now, they might hear you."

Why it would matter if those young'uns overheard what they were saying he didn't know or care about. Still he said, "I'm sorry." Annoying her wouldn't do. He'd come here for one reason and one reason only . . . to get his bonds back.

The wind settled to a gentle breeze, reminding Virgil of how peaceful the Adirondacks could be. But he'd never forget how cruel the area could be either. The weather here could change in an instant.

"What do you want, Virgil?"

A young boy and girl stepped out from behind the sheets. Virgil recognized them to be the same ones who'd been playing in the school yard. Remembering how the boy had fallen and scraped his knee, Virgil nodded to him. "How's your knee doing?"

"Nothing but a little scratch. Right, Miss Elsie?"

She didn't take her eyes off Virgil as she answered the boy. "Yes, Harry. Your knee is almost all healed."

Virgil had a feeling he'd best be getting to the reason for his visit. He said, "About that package you've been keeping for me?"

"Oh, for pity's sake! What on earth is so important about that envelope? I already told you I left it at my parents' house. I'll bring it here after church tomorrow. Is that time enough for you, Virgil?"

Her anger left him feeling jittery. He didn't need her to be getting all uppity with him. Not now, when he was in such dire straits. He shoved his hands in his front pants pockets.

"There's no need for you to shout at me."

"Virgil, after what you put me through, I'll shout at you if I want to!"

The little girl had come to stand in the folds of Elsie's skirt. She looked up at him wide-eyed, a thumb stuck in her mouth. Elsie brought her arm around the child, pulling her close to her side.

"Miss Elsie, do you need me to go find Uncle Will?" the boy asked, looking ready to defend her.

"No, Harry. I'm perfectly fine." She stared hard at Virgil.

He could see her pulse throbbing on the side of her neck. He had to gain control of this situation. And then he saw some of the tension drain from her face. She was looking past him. Turning around, he gave a start. Out of the shadows came a tall, dark-haired man. He wore his wide-brimmed hat low across his brow. In his arms he carried some short pieces of lumber and a length of thick roping.

The last time Virgil had seen him, the dark pants and sidearm had been covered by a long duster coat. Now though, standing here in the very clear light of day, Virgil recognized him to be the same man he'd seen snooping around his homestead a few weeks back. Looking from Elsie to this man, he wondered what was going on here.

"Uncle Will!" the boy called out and ran to his side.

Setting the wood and rope down, he reached out to pat the boy on the head. He said, "Harry, I see we have a visitor."

"Virgil Jensen, I'd like you to meet William Benton," Elsie said. "Mr. Benton works over at John Oliver's lumber company. These are his niece and nephew."

So that's what he's told her, that he works for John Oliver? Virgil felt the color drain from his face. "You are living here in the house with *him*?" He pointed in the man's direction.

"In separate living quarters."

Virgil shook his head. He didn't know this woman anymore. Why she would leave her family and move into town to take care of this man's family, he didn't know. But he knew for certain this man had told her he was a lumberjack, though Virgil felt it to the core of his being—William Benton wasn't who he said he was.

Elsie took him aside privately. "Virgil, I don't know what's gotten into you. I will get your things to you on Sunday. I promise."

The sweat rolled from underneath his hairline down his neck. Rubbing his hand along the shirt collar, he swiped away the wetness. He just wanted to get the bonds and leave Heartston. In hindsight, he realized he shouldn't have given them to Elsie in the first place. All this panic he'd been living with for the past few months had him making poor decisions. He'd get the bonds and sell them off. They could become someone else's worry. Since he'd found them, they'd brought him nothing but bad luck.

"Where should I meet you on Sunday?"

"You can meet me back here. Come after suppertime."

He wanted to tell her to get here sooner, but he knew better than to disagree with her. After all, his future now rested in her hands.

"All right. I'll be here tomorrow."

He fought the urge to look at Benton one more time. Keeping his head down, Virgil walked away. He overheard the man say to her, "Elsie, has Jensen been causing you trouble?" Quickening his pace, Virgil headed into town.

Chapter Thirteen

"No. Honestly, I don't know what's gotten into him."

Elsie bent over to pick up the empty laundry basket. She needed to get the children's laundry washed and hung out before the morning got away from her.

"Why did he come by?"

"He wants that envelope I told you about. I'll get it when I'm at my parents' house tomorrow, and then he can have it back." Looking past him, she saw the pile of supplies he'd been carrying lying in the grass.

Following her gaze, he said, "I'm going to put up some swings for the kids."

"Will! That's wonderful. Harry and Minnie, did you hear that? Your uncle is going to be putting up some swings for you!"

Rounding up the children, Will said, "Come on, I could use your help."

While Elsie went around the side of the house to wash the rest of the laundry, Will let Harry help him by handing him the tools he needed to get the project started. Winking at Minnie, he said, "You can let me know if I get the swings hanging straight."

As he worked, he thought about Virgil Jensen. Not at all what he expected from a man Elsie had been prepared to spend the rest of her life with. His clothes were tattered and worn. Though Virgil had clearly tried to wash up, Will had noticed smudges of dirt on the man's neck, cutting a groove along the inside of his shirt collar.

Something didn't sit right about the way the man had shifted from one foot to the other, his eyes darting from Will back to Elsie. And the tingling sensation at the base of Will's neck, the same one that had saved him many a time, had come back with a vengeance the minute he'd spotted good ole Virgil in the yard.

Even Elsie and the children had appeared on guard.

"Uncle Will?"

"What?"

"You really gonna climb this tree?"

The three of them were standing underneath an old oak tree where Will planned to hang the swings. Its long, thick branches spread wide over the front yard. In a few weeks the leaves would fill in and shade the walkway and porch in coolness, protecting them from the summer heat.

Holding the lengths of rope in his hands, Will eyed a thick branch protruding from the center of the tree. "Yup."

Craning his neck, Harry peered up. "That's really high. You might fall."

Will followed Harry's gaze. It really wasn't any higher than ten feet. He imagined to a small child the distance seemed mighty high. "I'll be fine," he said as he found a foothold in the large tree trunk.

Carefully he pulled himself up into the V of the tree, the place where the branches grew outward. Shimmying across the first sturdy branch he came to, Will stopped halfway out on the limb. Pushing himself up into a sitting position, he dropped the first swing over the side. Then he tied the thick ropes into place. From his perch he realized he could see all the way down Heartston's main street.

Since it was Saturday, the town was bustling with people hurrying to do their errands. A line of customers spilled out onto the sidewalk in front of Amy's bake shop, and the door to the post office opened and closed every few minutes with people picking up their weekly mail delivery. A gentle breeze carried the tinny sounds of the out-of-tune saloon piano. The swinging doors pushed open and out staggered Elsie's former beau.

"Well, I'll be . . ." Will's voice trailed off. He heard Elsie call and quickly turned his attention to her.

"William Benton! You better pay attention to what you're doing!"

Looking down at her standing there with her hands planted firmly on her hips, with strands of her dark hair dancing in the breeze, he thought she was the prettiest sight he'd ever laid eyes upon.

After tying the last of the knots, he shimmied down the branch and, resting his foot in the V of the tree trunk, hopped down to join her. The children ran to their swings, clearly delighted by his handiwork. He stepped closer to Elsie and, seeing her fidgeting with her hair, found himself unable to resist the urge to touch the silken strand she struggled with. Reaching out his hand, he took the lock from between her fingers and gently tucked it behind her ear.

Her lips parted as she stilled. Looking down into her magnificent violet eyes, their color bringing to mind the wonders of springtime, he saw them darken. A light blush rode high on her cheekbones.

Behind them laughter spilled from the children. Bees droned along the length of the forsythia hedge. The plant's thin branches blossomed with buttercup-yellow flowers. Off in the distance the piercing train whistle echoed off the mountains. All Will could think about was Elsie's pretty mouth. He move to stand toe to toe with her.

And all those sounds faded into the background until the only thing he heard was her soft intake of breath. Bending his head, he touched her mouth with his. She tasted like warm honey. Her lips pressed against his. Wrapping his arms around her, Will gently drew her into him. To his utter surprise and delight, their kiss deepened until he felt Elsie's hands pressing against his chest.

Lifting his head, he waited for her recriminations. But again she surprised him.

"That was . . ." Her words trailed away.

"Nice." He finished for her. He watched as the blush on her face deepened. But she held his gaze steady, searching his face. Hoping to find what, he didn't know. She laid her hand gently alongside his cheek. Her fingertips felt cool against the heat of his weather-worn skin.

He heard the steam spraying from the train engine as it pulled to a stop at the station, the sound an intrusion bringing him back to reality. To him their kiss had seemed like an eternity, when in fact it had only been a moment in time. He wondered what Elsie was thinking.

"Will, you shouldn't have kissed me."

"Why not?"

"We're out here in the open. What would the neighbors think if they saw us?"

"I'm sorry. The next time I kiss you, I'll make sure we're inside away from all those prying eyes." Because one thing was for sure, Will would be kissing her again.

He saw a spark of mischief in her eyes, but she turned her attention to the twins. Harry was trying to teach Minnie how to pump her legs to move the swing on her own.

With Elsie leading the way, they went to help Harry.

Minnie clung to the ropes as Harry pushed her. She seemed irritated by his efforts, her mouth screwed up in a tight line of frustration.

Elsie took the empty swing, placing her backside snuggly on the flat wooden seat. "Minnie, watch me."

With great exaggeration, Elsie swung her legs out straight and then pumped them hard back underneath the swing. Her skirts fluttered to and fro in the breeze her movement created. Before long, Elsie was soaring to Will's height. He caught a glimpse of her silk stockings. Seeing where he was looking, she sucked in her lower lip. He suspected she wanted to keep his prying eyes away, but then he saw that little glint appear in her eyes and her mouth turned upward.

"You try, Minnie." Elsie slowed her momentum so that Minnie could watch her.

Minnie began to slowly move her legs, and before long, she joined Elsie soaring into the air.

Bringing the swing to a stop, Elsie said, "You did a fine job, Minnie." She hopped off. "I've got to get back to my chores."

Will walked with her to the house. Casting a sidelong glance toward her, he could see faint lines of fatigue around her eyes. Elsie had been working long hours. He didn't imagine that teaching all day and then caring for the household and for the children was easy on her. But she never complained. He felt certain she never would. Elsie wasn't one to lament about things.

Picking up the empty wicker laundry basket, he walked with her to the side yard where the wash bin had been set up. They hadn't talked about Virgil's visit yet.

Setting the basket down against the back door stoop, he said, "I want to be here when Virgil comes by tomorrow."

"Will, while I appreciate your intentions, Virgil is truly harmless." Taking a pair of dark pants from the wash water, she fed them through the fat rolls of the ringer.

"Just the same. You let me know when he gets here."

She fed one of Minnie's dresses through the contraption. "Are you planning on joining us for church services tomorrow?"

Rubbing a hand along the base of his neck, Will wanted to tell her no. But they'd been making some good headway lately, and he didn't want to risk ruining that by telling her he probably would not be going with them tomorrow. Instead, he offered, "Why don't you take a break?"

"For land's sakes, today is the only day I have to get this wash done. And then I have to bake cookies because tomorrow I'm signed up to bring those for after-church refreshments."

Laying his hand over hers, he forced her to stop fidgeting. "Elsie, you do too much around here as it is. Why not take an hour to rest up a bit?"

"Tomorrow is time enough for a day off." Turning her back to him, she worked at getting the rest of the wash wrung out.

He was heading around to the wood pile when her words stopped him.

"Will, the kiss . . ."

Folding his arms across his chest, he grinned at her, waiting to hear her thoughts. She sure was fussing with the shirt she held in her hands, twisting it around so much that he didn't think it would need to go through the wringer. Will stepped closer and, cradling her face in his hands, bent in and kissed her again.

She broke away from his touch. "Will. You need to stop doing that."

"Doing what?" He liked teasing her.

"Kissing me."

"Don't you like it?"

"I do and that's the problem. I'm here to take care of your house and the children. These kisses complicate that."

Maybe he'd gone too far or acted too quickly. It didn't matter because, to him, kissing Elsie felt right. And it had been a long time since anything in his life had felt so right.

"I gave my heart to Virgil and he just left me. I don't want that to happen again."

"I'm not Virgil."

"I know you're not. But you've never settled down, either. Not until you had your niece and nephew handed to you a few months back. Will, I know you were not even considering settling down before then. You came to Heartston for this job. Nothing more. You told me so yourself."

"A man can change."

He said those words realizing them to be true. Whether he'd wanted it to or been expecting it, Will's life had changed over these past months. He'd gone from being a loner to having the responsibility of taking care of Harry and Minnie. And yes, even the stubborn, independent Elsie Mitchell needed him. She may not want to admit it just yet, but he could tell by the way she waited up for him or held supper for him those nights when he had been working late at the lumberyard.

Their lives were becoming intertwined, and when the time came, he wasn't sure he'd be able to simply walk away. He blinked in surprise. "A man can change." He repeated those words to himself.

And hadn't she heard the same tune—"A man can change"—from Virgil? After seeing the desperation in that man earlier today, Elsie didn't think he would ever change his ways. As for Will, deep in her heart she suspected that there was a lot more to what made up William Benton than he ever let on. If he would open himself to her fully, maybe then she could consider more than just the kisses.

In her heart of hearts she realized she did want more from him. But she didn't think she could bear the hurt and pain if Will ended up leaving her as Virgil had. Elsie had never been the kind of woman who issued ultimatums, but she was sorely tempted to do so with Will.

"Elsie. Tell me what you're thinking?"

She took a good hard look into his eyes. He gave her a half smile. But he didn't fool her. Elsie thought Will was very good at masking his true feelings. She knew he loved Harry and Minnie and recognized that he didn't give out that feeling freely or easily. She also knew him to be very loyal and a good, hard worker. But that didn't make it wise for her to give her heart to him.

And yet that was exactly what she found herself wanting to do. She'd grown used to their life here in town. Some days she even found herself daydreaming that they really were a family. And then she'd be reminded of her commitment to the town as its schoolteacher. Or she would look in the mirror and realize that she was no longer considered to be of marrying age. Why would a man like Will want to be with her? Those concerns had been one of the reasons she'd begun to pursue her dreams of travel.

She wanted him to join them in the family pew for church services of his own volition. She didn't want to be disappointed by his absences at the dinner table anymore. She couldn't say those words. Instead, she said, "I'm thinking it's turned out to be a fine day to hang out the wash."

Narrowing his eyes, he put his hands on his hips. "You're not thinking that at all."

"Will. Why do you want to know my feelings? Why is this so important to you now?"

"Because whether or not you or I ever intended it to happen . . . we've been making a home here for Harry and Minnie."

Suddenly she felt like they were living the Bible story where two men are tasked with building houses. One builds his on sand and the other on solid rock. Only the home built on rock could withstand the storm. She feared the "sand" foundation they'd been building their lives upon would never hold up to the storm yet to come.

"This is a home for them. We knew it would never be for all of us."

"I know what our agreement was, Elsie. Let me ask you this: How long had you planned to go on living here?"

"I don't know. I guess until you decided my services were no longer needed." Tears sprung to her eyes. "Are you asking me to leave?"

He came to her then, taking her into his arms. She heard his intake of breath, could feel the solid, steady beat of his heart beneath her ear.

His voice whispered, "I'm not asking you to leave."

Picking her head up off the hard wall of his chest, she wanted to know, "Then what are you asking?"

The wind picked up again, grabbing at her hair, pulling the strands loose. Will rescued them, wrapping the long lengths around a finger. "I'm not sure."

"I'm not sure I can risk my heart again." Her words caught in the wind, and she wasn't sure if Will heard what she'd said. He sighed against her, making Elsie wonder if she'd gone too far with her honesty.

Afraid of what she might find in his eyes, Elsie averted her gaze from his, instead looking around his shoulder to where the children were still playing on their swings. Realizing that their entire relationship had been based on Harry and Minnie didn't make her feel any better. Whatever happened between them would affect the twins. Eventually, he moved ever so slightly away from her.

"No one knows what tomorrow will bring."

"I have faith that tomorrow will come." She felt her mouth loosening from the tense hold it had been in.

"Then I think you should have faith in us." He grinned down at her. "Let's just agree to leave it at that for right now."

"I suppose I can do that."

"Oh, and Elsie, I will be here tomorrow when Virgil returns."

Chapter Fourteen

She finally gave in to Will's insistence of her need for a break. Leaving him at the house, she wandered into the village, finding it hard to believe that so much time had passed since she'd had a chance to visit with her friend Amy. Coming to a stop in front of the bakery, she noticed the "Closed" sign had been posted. She hoped to find Amy still there and knocked on the door.

Amy opened the door, a cleaning cloth in hand. "What a lovely surprise!" Beaming, she gave Elsie a warm hug. "Elsie! It's been ages since I've seen you!"

"I know. I'm so sorry for not getting here sooner." She returned the hug.

Amy brought her back into the kitchen. Once there, she directed Elsie to a chair. "Sit here while I make us some tea."

Not used to being waited on, Elsie offered to help. "At least let me get the cups and saucers."

Amy pointed to the usual shelf where the tea set sat. Elsie took the china service down and brought the teapot to where Amy had set the kettle to boiling on the stove.

"Did you hear the news? My parents are going to be returning home!"

"Oh, Amy! That's wonderful news. You must be so happy."

"I am. While I enjoy running the bakery, it's a lot of long hours." Waving a hand in front of her heart-shaped face, she added, "I'm not complaining, mind you."

"I understand. Still, it is a lot of work and responsibility running a business by yourself." Elsie thought about how hard she worked and was thankful for Will's occasional help.

Once she had the tea leaves brewing in the pot and scones on a plate, Amy nudged Elsie over to the small round table. "Come on, let's sit down and enjoy our teatime."

"Tell me, when are you expecting your parents to arrive?"

"My mother's last letter said they'd be in Heartston within the month."

"That's good to hear."

Amy put her hand on Elsie's. "Tell me how you're doing with the children and Mr. Benton."

"He kissed me!" She blurted out the words.

Amy's mouth dropped open, and then she snapped it shut. "My, my, this is interesting news."

"I'm not sure how I feel about it."

"Didn't you like it?"

"His kiss was wonderful. A bit of a surprise."

"Tell me everything."

Elsie proceeded to explain the day to her friend. "Virgil came by while I was hanging out the wash. There's something not right about him, Amy. I'm worried about him."

"I heard he'd returned and that he's been staying out at his parents' old homestead. Frankly, I don't think you should trouble yourself with him. Why was he there?"

"He came for the envelope."

"I say give it to him and be finished with the scoundrel for good."

"I would, except I left it back at my parents' house. And as I was telling him this, Mr. Benton came home."

"Go on."

"I'm afraid I raised my voice and frightened the children. Harry was about to run off to find his uncle." She remembered how safe she'd felt when Will had walked into the side yard.

"Sounds to me like Mr. Benton came home at just the right time."

"I was glad to see him. Not that I think Virgil would do any physical harm to me, but it was a relief to have a man there just in case."

"When did this kiss happen?"

"While I was finishing the laundry, after Mr. Benton had hung up new swings for the children."

"Sounds to me like things are moving along nicely between the two of you."

"I never expected to have feelings like these again, Amy. I figured after Virgil and with my age and all that no man would be interested."

"Don't you dare say such a thing! You're a beautiful woman inside and out. You're smart, too. And look at the wonders you've worked on those children. They adore you. So it seems to me William Benton is a smart man to be interested in you."

Elsie blushed. She wished it were that simple.

"Amy, I really know very little about his past."

"Does that matter?"

"It's just that sometimes he goes out and returns late into the night or not at all."

"Perhaps he's doing work for John over at one of the lumber camps."

Toying with the teacup handle, she thought Amy could be right. But that wasn't her only concern.

"He frequents the saloon."

Amy raised her eyebrows. "I know the men who work at the camps come into town just to go to the saloon. Could it be possible he's socializing with them?"

"I suppose so. He did mention he went there for business purposes."

"Elsie, I get the feeling that he is not the type to take advantage of all the saloon's services."

"You're right. And he's never smelled of alcohol. Just nasty cigar smoke."

But deep down she could tell Will was keeping something from her . . . holding back a part of himself. She'd learned her lesson the hard way with Virgil. She wouldn't give herself to another man unless she knew for certain he could come to her freely. Elsie didn't want to believe that Will could be doing things she would never be able to accept. Keeping secrets from those you cared about never served anyone well.

"I'm tired of fretting about my relationship with Will. How are things going with you and Mr. Oliver?"

Amy's face lit up. "He's been by nearly every day for the past two weeks. Comes by at the same time every morning for a scone and coffee."

"I'm glad to hear this. Has he come to his senses and realized that you've been pining after him?"

Amy laughed. "I think he knows." She looked down at the empty plate, saying, "He's asked me to join him for a day at one of the Great Camps."

Clapping her hands together, Elsie exclaimed, "I'm so happy for you!"

"Thank you. I've waited a long time for him to take notice. I'm afraid our outing will have to wait until after my parents' return, though. There's no one to look after the shop."

"It won't be long. You said so yourself they'll be here within the month. By then the roads will be dried from the melting snow and spring runoff. You'll be able to enjoy the trip. And in the meantime you can enjoy your morning visits with Mr. Oliver."

"I'm so glad you stopped by today, Elsie. You've helped put some of my worries at ease. As for you and Will, I feel like it's all going to work out."

Rising from the chair, she helped Amy clean up their tea dishes. After they were finished, she hugged her friend good-bye and walked back home. Will had been right, a few hours away did wonders to rejuvenate her. Now she felt ready to finish the chores.

She paused in front of the house, her breath caught in her throat. Laying her hand against the base of her neck, she looked at the scene before her, finding it almost impossible to believe that a few short months ago this house had been vacant.

Where emptiness had once been, life now pulsed blissfully along. She took in the rockers on the porch and the swings swaying happily in the breeze. From where she stood, she could just make out the edge of the vegetable garden Will and Harry had so lovingly planted. Around back, the sheets she'd hung out this morning flapped, dried by the wind.

She could hear Will's voice speaking in gentle tones. Moving closer, she realized he was reading aloud to Harry and Minnie. They sat on the top step of the back stoop. Will sat between them with the book resting on his lap. Minnie had one arm looped through the crook of Will's elbow, and Harry was using his finger to follow the words along the page as Will read them.

She didn't recognize the book. She could see a picture of a train on the cover. It didn't matter what the book was because at that very moment Elsie felt her heart bursting with so much contentment, so much love for the children, for this home they were creating. And for Will. She knew without a doubt, no matter what happened, that she wanted this to last forever.

Elsie decided the kisses from Will were just the beginning of wonderful things to come for them. She now believed the Lord had brought them together to make a home for Harry and Minnie, and more importantly for them to find each other. But how could she make this her future with Will when he seemed so reluctant to open his heart and mind to fully accepting the Lord into his life? She knew he had faith, she just had to get him to trust in that. And there was this unfinished business with Virgil gnawing away at her. She needed to settle things with that man once and for all.

Elsie had to find a way to put everything right.

Finally coming to the end of the story, Will looked up at her. "Did you have a nice visit with Amy?" he asked.

"Now, how did you know that's where I went?"

Leaving the book with Minnie, he stood. "It's where you always go when you're in need of a good friend to talk to."

"Amy's parents are going to be coming home soon. She's very excited about seeing them again." Stepping around Will, she retrieved the laundry basket from where she'd left it at the back door.

He accompanied her to the wash line, where she began taking down the sheets.

"The children seemed to be enjoying your storybook."

He helped her with the sheets.

"I bought it for Harry to replace the one his aunt Mary Beth took from him. I probably should get a special book for Minnie, too." He frowned. "When do you suppose she's going to talk to us?"

"Soon, I hope. I pray for her every day." Stacking the last folded sheet on top of the full basket, she added, "She'll come around."

"I don't know if I have the patience like you do to wait for that day to come."

Watching him pick up the basket, she replied, "You need to leave it in the hands of the Lord and believe that when the time is right, Minnie will find her voice again. Will, if you could just trust in him and trust in me when I tell you your faith can carry you through even the most unimaginably hard times."

Just as she thought he might, Will didn't respond. Instead, he turned and walked up the back steps into the kitchen, leaving the basket by the table. It was as if a dark cloud had descended on them. His entire demeanor changed. She could see him closing himself off from her like he'd done so many times before. She longed to reach out to him, to touch him, to hold him close.

"Tell me what caused you to lose faith, Will. Please."

"Elsie," he warned. "This is not a subject I wish to discuss."

"Maybe you should."

"Let's just say I've traveled around a lot and seen the things people do to one another." He shrugged. "Their actions have left me thinking that sometimes faith isn't enough to get a person through life."

"Oh, Will! You've never been more wrong."

"I need to go into town for a while."

She stilled. And then she started tapping her toe. Why wouldn't he tell her what he was thinking and feeling?

"Will, you just have to turn to the Lord again."

He shook his head. When Elsie reached her hand out to try and touch his arm, he took a step back.

"I have work that needs tending to over at the lumberyard."

She knew he wasn't being truthful with her. Determination and pride kept her from calling him on the fact. "Should I wait on supper for you?" she asked.

"Don't hold it for me."

Will walked away from the house feeling like the biggest of cads. But the moment he'd seen Elsie's face, he knew he had to get to the bottom of the bond thievery as soon as possible. He wanted to close the case. He couldn't move forward until this job was finished. Being a Pinkerton had been his life for so many years. Will could barely imagine not doing this job. How could he possibly fit someone like Elsie into his life? He also knew Elsie's strong feelings about the church and her faith. She deserved a man who could give her the world she desired. And that man was not him.

He heard the ruckus even before he came in sight of the saloon. The closer he got, the greater the feel of the tension filling the air became. Stepping between two lumberjacks, he elbowed his way into the room. Here the din was much louder. He squinted his eyes, looking through the brown haze of cigar smoke into the crowd, until his attention fixed on one man.

Dwarfed by the dozen or so lumberjacks standing around him in a loose circle, Virgil Jensen had one hand in his pocket while another gripped the handle of a beer mug so tightly Will could see the whites of his knuckles. He could make out the grumblings of a few of the men. Seemed there was a poker game about to start. Virgil wanted in.

"You still owe me for your last game," a tall, burly man snarled. Will recognized him from the lumber camp.

He saw Virgil reach into his pocket and pull out a thin roll of bills. It didn't look like there was enough there to cover his debt and the next game. He was curious about how and if Virgil would get himself out of this mess. Deciding to keep his distance, Will stepped away from the group. He glanced toward the stage where the next show would be starting.

The sound of dozens of voices swirled around him, mingling with loud laughter and the occasional cheer as the dancing girls started assembling in a line along the low stage placed at one end of the narrow room. Candlelit sconces were set up in a row at the edge of the stage, casting the girls in hazy light. Their long shadows swayed on the wall behind them. Making his way to the bar, Will got his usual—a glass of dark ale—which both he and the bartender knew Will wouldn't touch. He laid a coin in the bartender's hand. The bartender inclined his head in the direction of the stage. Turning, Will rested his elbow on the bar and looked over the heads of the lumberjacks just in time to catch Lily lowering her head. Will followed her gaze. He saw Virgil still standing in the mix of men.

Virgil shifted from foot to foot. His eyes were wide, and he looked afraid. Virgil's wild gaze shifted between the doorway behind them and the man standing in front of him with his hand out. Will couldn't tell if he was more afraid of the men or of not getting in on the game.

The pieces of the puzzle Will had been fighting to solve were all falling into place. Virgil had a gambling problem.

The piano player started up a loud, upbeat dance tune that set the girls in motion. Their mid-calf-length skirts swirled and waved around their legs, riding above their knees to show off their frilly, thigh-high garters.

As Lily danced in step with the saloon girls, Virgil's little group of men moved through the crowd, going through a side door. Leaving his beer on the bar, Will followed them. As he moved quietly through the narrow, dimly lit hallway, he stopped in front of a single door. On the other side he heard the men talking in low voices. Virgil kept assuring them that he had the money to ante up. When he was about to be tossed out for his lie, Will pushed through the doorway.

Reaching into his coat pocket, he pulled out a wad of money. Tossing the bills on the table in front of Virgil, he said, "I've got him covered."

Virgil's face lost all color as he stared up, recognizing his benefactor. At first glance, Will expected the weasel to bolt from the room. Instead, he reached out with a surprisingly steady hand and gathered the money in front of him on the table. After Will assured the group he was just there as an observer, he stepped back into the shadows, finding a spot along the wall to rest his back against.

The winnings of the first few hands were split evenly with the five players, which didn't come as a surprise to Will. Most of the men had so many tells that even an amateur could spot them. He listened as the music out in the saloon changed from a quick tempo to a lighter one.

The cheers died down. Will assumed the women had finished their show. He waited for Lily to come to him.

In the meantime, he watched as Virgil started losing hand after hand, until just one coin remained in his stash. Recognizing the signs of a gambling compulsion, Will thought it no surprise that he'd broken off his engagement with Elsie. The man clearly needed this to survive. While most of the men were gathering up their winnings, Virgil remained at the table, running the coin through his fingers. The last man looked across the table and cocked an eyebrow. Virgil nodded. The man dealt out another hand of five-card stud.

It was hard for Will to remain silent at his post. He wanted to reach out and throttle some sense into Virgil. But he knew it would do no good. Virgil was so far gone, and Will seriously doubted anyone could make him see the error of his ways. Will sent up a prayer of thanksgiving that Elsie hadn't married Virgil. Knowing how strongly devoted she was to her friends and family, he feared she would have stayed with this man to the bitter end.

Virgil had done the right thing by leaving her.

A light tap on his shoulder had him look behind him. Lily had slipped unnoticed into the room. She inclined her head, and Will followed her out into the dark hallway.

"What do you have for me?"

"Virgil has been in the saloon all day. He came in as soon as Hal unlocked the doors. I heard him tell one of the girls that he was going to be leaving town soon."

"Did he mention where he'd be going?"

"No. But he said something about getting back some papers he'd left with a friend of his." Lily tugged the front of her saloon dress up in an effort to cover herself. "Why do I always have to be the saloon girl?"

"Because I wouldn't look as good as you do in that getup."

She swatted his arm. "Virgil Jensen is big on whatever those papers are, Will. He said getting them back could be a matter of life or death."

"From the looks of him, I'd guess he's left a trail of debtors. Maybe those papers are worth enough to pay off his obligations and then some. There's only one thing I can think of right now that might be so valuable."

She leaned in toward him, lowering her voice as a pair of drunken lumberjacks stumbled past them, going out the back door into the alleyway. "Some stolen railroad bonds perhaps?"

The timing fit. Virgil had been in the Albany area at the time of the bond theft. Elsie had already told Will how she'd met Virgil while visiting her aunt and uncle. He'd given her a package. A whoosh of humid air rolled down the hallway as the back door opened and closed.

Will rolled his shoulders, trying to get rid of the nagging tension stuck between his shoulder blades. From the way he'd been playing that game in there, Virgil was getting desperate. And if Will knew one thing about desperation, it could make a person do things they'd never thought about before. If Elsie had those bonds, she was in danger. Harry and Minnie could be in danger, too.

Lily must have been thinking along the same lines because she said, "You've got to follow him. I'm afraid I can't. The girls are probably wondering where I am right now. I told them I needed a break from the noise. The men seem to be a bit bawdier than usual tonight."

"Take care of yourself, Lily. I don't want to see anything happen to you."

"Now don't you be worrying about me, Will. Remember, I've got my best friend strapped right here against my leg within easy reach if I need him." Lily grinned into the dimness of the hallway, patting the spot high up on her leg where she kept a small pearl-handled revolver.

Will chuckled. "I wouldn't want to be on the receiving end of your wrath, Agent Handland." Becoming serious, he added, "Look after Elsie and the children for me. I'm going to be tracking Virgil from here on out."

"Is there something I should know about, Will?"

"Like what?"

"Like are you finally falling in love with something, or should I say someone, other than this job?"

He shook his head.

The door to the hallway opened again. One of the saloon girls called out to Lily. "I need to be getting back."

He watched her move through the doorway into the saloon. He reentered the dark room where the poker game had been played to find only the dealer left at the table. His head was slumped over and Will heard him snore. Laying a hand on his shoulder, he gave him a quick shake, waking him up.

"Hey. Where's the man who was sitting across from you?"

Chapter Fifteen

"He left."

"Do you know where he went?"

"Nope. Now leave me in peace so I can get some shut-eye. I gotta go clean up that mess in a bit."

Will headed back out into the saloon hall. Looking around the room, he didn't see any sign of Virgil. At the bar, he gave the barkeep a description of the man. The barkeep informed him he'd left a few minutes ago. Virgil was probably heading back to his family homestead. But Will worried he might backtrack to see Elsie again. Leaving the saloon, he stepped out into the humid air. Off in the distance he could see flashes of lightning illuminating the mountain peaks. Thunder rumbled. The first spring storm lit up the night sky. Picking up his pace, he hurried to the house.

Standing in the shadows of a lilac bush, he looked at the house. He saw a flicker of candlelight moving from the kitchen into the parlor. Elsie's silhouette appeared at the front window. The curtain moved as she peered out into the darkness.

Will wanted to go inside and confess everything to her. He yearned to tell her the truth . . . to free himself from the subterfuge he'd been living in for so long. But he couldn't do that. Confessing could bring harm to her and the children. Once this assignment was complete, he'd tell her who he really was. And if her faith in the Lord and life was as good as she claimed, she'd understand why he'd done the things he'd done.

He watched her light a lantern and then set it on the roll top desk. He'd come home many a night to find the welcoming light left on for him. He watched her walk through the doorway into the kitchen. The candlelight moved through the room and into her quarters until it disappeared.

Satisfied that Virgil wasn't there, Will went over to the livery to get a horse. Rousting the watchman, he had him get the black gelding. Then he set off for the Jensen place. More thunder rumbled, spooking the horse. He pulled on the reins, controlling the animal. "There, there, boy. It's just a storm, nothing more. Just the angels in heaven bowling."

The words stilled his movements. He closed his eyes against a memory so vivid it made his heart ache. His mother had told him he shouldn't fear the thunderstorms because they were nothing more than God letting the angels play.

Up ahead a bolt of lightning shot through the sky, splitting open the darkness. The horse shied.

Sliding from the saddle, Will took the reins in one hand, patting the horse's fear-dampened neck. "I promise you, boy, there's nothing to be afraid of."

He led the horse along an old overgrown pathway. It didn't take them long to come to the edge of the Jensen homestead. Will used the next flash of light to look for any signs that Virgil had been here. Off to one side of the pathway, he saw a few spots where the grass had been trampled down.

Still leading the horse, he ventured farther onto the property. He could just make out a trail of smoke coming up the dilapidated chimney. Light flickered from the center of the house. Virgil had come home.

The air stilled as the storms moved around the sky. Perhaps the rain would come and break the humidity. Or maybe the storms would eventually move out. Either way, Will would be here waiting, watching. Sooner or later Virgil was going to get what he'd come back to Heartston for. Wanting to make this a solid case, he needed to catch Virgil red-handed with those bonds in his possession.

Elsie, being true to her word, would be going out to her parents' house to retrieve Virgil's stuff tomorrow after the church service. He felt certain the bonds were there. Beside him the horse pawed at the ground, then finding a bit of grass, nibbled away on it.

He suspected Virgil was feeling a bit overzealous since he'd promised those men back at the saloon that he could pay off his debt. There was nothing worse than a desperate person. Will needed to be on the watch for what Virgil might do the next day. Taking an oilskin duster from his saddlebag, Will found a spot underneath a pine tree. He sat facing the house. Pulling the coat around his shoulders, he settled in for the night.

The sound of the rain splashing against the window pane woke Elsie. Lying there with her head against the soft feather pillow, she listened to the sounds of the house. It was quiet. She'd tried to wait up for Will last night, but the hour had grown so late. She'd finally given up and, leaving the lantern burning low in the front parlor, gone to bed.

She'd been silly to think that after the kisses they'd shared that he would stop his late nights at work. If indeed that was where he'd been going. She thought about the last time he'd stayed out till all hours, coming home reeking of the saloon.

Realizing she wasn't going to fall back to sleep, she found her robe at the end of the bed and put it on. Tying the sash tightly around her waist, she wandered out into the kitchen to begin the day's chores.

The lamp's flame still sputtered on the low setting. Will hadn't come home again. Frowning, she went into the parlor to blow out the flame. After all that had passed between them yesterday, she had thought Will was changing—that things between them were changing.

The wind slammed the rain against the front windows, rattling the panes so hard she feared they might blow out. She turned at the sound of Harry and Minnie scurrying down the stairs, frightened by the storm.

"Miss Elsie, the wind is blowing something fierce!" Harry exclaimed.

"The storm is fast moving, it should blow through soon, I suspect. Let's go into the kitchen and get some breakfast." Putting her arms around each of them, she herded them into the kitchen.

While the children sat at the table, she made up some oatmeal and heated the tea water.

"Where's Uncle Will?" Harry asked, fidgeting with his spoon and napkin.

"He's working."

"I tried to wait up for him, but I was so tired after playing outside on our swings. Will the rain hurt the plants in the garden?"

"No. The rain will help them grow." Distracting him from the whereabouts of his uncle, she asked, "Tell me what you'd like in your oatmeal."

"Some of those dried apples and maple syrup. Minnie wants the same for hers."

Taking the dried apples down from the pantry shelf, she said, "Harry, we need to let Minnie start to answer for herself."

She was surprised to turn around and find a stricken-looking Harry staring back at her.

"No. She needs me to talk for her."

Setting the container of apples down on the table, Elsie pulled out a chair and sat. Looking at Harry and then Minnie, she explained, "I know you've been through a hard time, losing your parents the way you did, and I can only imagine how much the pain has hurt you on the inside."

Harry's eyes brimmed with unshed tears, while Minnie hugged Hazel close, making Elsie wish she hadn't started this conversation. But the fact of the matter was that living here in Heartston with their uncle was their life now. She wanted to help Minnie move through her pain. To show her that life here could be wonderful.

Though she didn't want them to forget their parents, she did want them to feel loved and nurtured. Reaching out, she covered Harry's hands with hers, wishing with all her heart that their uncle were here. Will needed to be a part of this conversation.

"Some days I miss my ma and pa so much I feel an ache right here." Harry pointed to the spot on his chest where his heart lay. "I know they're in heaven just like you've told us. Sometimes I even feel like my mamma is watching over us. Does that sound strange to you, Miss Elsie?"

Elsie felt his heartache. She gave his hand a gentle squeeze. "It sounds perfectly wonderful to me, Harry. Not strange at all."

A loud clap of thunder and then a bolt of lightning sent the children straight into her arms.

She reassured them there was nothing to fear. Mother Nature was just making her presence known. She gave thanks for the distraction, even if the noise from the storm did vibrate through the walls of the house.

She thought about Will and where he'd gotten off to. And she hoped he could remain safely out of the storm, because when he did get himself back home, they were going to have a set-to. Never one to stay in limbo for too long, Elsie felt the time had come for them to make a decision about their future. Leaving the children at their seats, she finished putting breakfast on the table. The storm eventually died down, moving on over the mountain peaks.

She had a busy day ahead. She bustled about the kitchen getting the dishes cleaned and put away. Then she ushered Harry and Minnie upstairs to get dressed for church. Once they were set, she left them reading from their favorite storybook in the parlor.

Because they would be making their way to church along the muddy roadway, Elsie decided to wear one of her older church gowns, a light tan. She placed her bonnet atop her head, tying the green grosgrain ribbon underneath her chin.

They set off to Sunday services. As she watched her fellow parishioners enter the sanctuary, she wished for Will to appear.

The service seemed long to her. Elsie had to fight to stay focused. Her mind kept wandering to Will and what he might be doing. After the service ended, she joined her parents out in the churchyard.

"I thought the children and I might accompany you home."

"Your father and I have accepted a dinner invitation from the postmaster and his wife. We won't be going back home until later this afternoon."

"If it's all right with you, I'd like to take the children out there anyway. I need to pick something up. Besides, I'm sure they'd enjoy getting out of town for a bit."

"Take our wagon. The roads are still muddy and wet from the thunderstorms. Just leave it at your house, and we'll pick it up on our way out of town later," her father said.

"That's a fine idea. Thank you, Father." She kissed her mother and father good-bye, then loaded Harry and Minnie in the back of the wagon.

Seeing the puddles in the rutted roadway stretching out of town, Elsie was glad her father had offered to let her take the wagon. They arrived at the house a short time later to find the chickens ranging about the yard, happily clucking and pecking at the ground.

"Miss Elsie, can we go see if there are any eggs?" Harry leapt from the back of the wagon before she could offer to help him down.

"Do you remember where to find the basket?"

"Hanging on the outside of the chicken coop."

Smiling, she watched as Harry and Minnie ran off toward the barn. She tied the mare to the hitching post and made her way into the main room of the house she'd grown up in. It seemed strange after all the years she'd spent here to be stopping by for visits. Untying her bonnet, she left it on the entryway table. The familiar scent of the lemon-and-herb potpourri that her mother kept in a bowl on the table filled her with memories of another time, when her entire life was here in this house—a house filled with love and affection.

Moving through the parlor, she walked down the short hallway to the staircase that led to the two bedrooms upstairs. Hers was the one tucked up under the front eave of the house. She put her foot on the first step, then paused. The floorboard above her creaked. Bewildered by the noise, she looked up, thinking perhaps the house was groaning from the wind. Gathering her skirts, she continued up the staircase, coming to a sudden stop right outside her bedroom door.

The door had been left half-open. She could hear a scraping sound. Wood against wood. Someone was in her room! She slammed the door open. It hit the wall with a loud thud.

"What on earth are you doing?"

A man spun around.

She gasped. "Virgil!"

"Now don't be getting upset with me, Elsie. I told you I needed that envelope."

"And I told you that I would bring it to you later today." Seeing him standing in her bedroom, knowing that he'd entered her parents' house like a common criminal, left her spitting mad.

"Get out this instant!"

"I can't do that."

Taking two steps into the room, she said, "You can, and you will do as I ask."

He shook his head, sending long, greasy locks of hair swinging across his shoulders. He wore gloves and the same clothes he'd had on yesterday. Looking down the length of him, she noticed his boots were caked in mud. *Of course they would be,* she thought, because she hadn't seen any sign of a horse or wagon outside. He must have walked through the rain-soaked land the five miles from his parents' place.

Thinking back on it, she realized he hadn't come by on horseback yesterday, either. *What had happened to him over the years? What had made him enter her family's home uninvited?*

"Virgil, let me help you."

"Where's the envelope, Elsie?"

She moved toward him, closer, so close she could now see the hardness in his eyes. The first quiver of fear ran along her spine. She could hear Harry and Minnie making their way back from the henhouse. She wanted to warn them to stay outside. She bit back a warning as Virgil took a menacing step toward her.

"Don't open your mouth, Elsie. I'll get what's mine and be gone before those young'uns even get to the porch. Now where's my packet?"

"Your stuff is right there in the top drawer of my dresser." She started toward the dresser. "Virgil, what's happened to you?"

"Don't try to distract me with your words of concern. I know how you feel about me. I've seen the way you and your man look at each other."

"You're talking about Will?"

He nodded. "Get me what I came here for."

She pulled open the top drawer of her dresser. Lifting a scarf, she felt around underneath the fabric. The envelope wasn't there. *Where could it be?* She'd left it right here. Maybe she was mistaken. Perhaps she'd put it in the next drawer. Her fingers trembled as she went to the second drawer.

"Where is it?" Virgil moved toward her.

She saw him reach around his back.

"I need the envelope now!" He pulled out a gun, pointing it at Elsie. "Are you waiting for him?"

She shook her head.

"I think you are."

She heard the children coming into the house. Elsie was afraid of what Virgil might do to them. She had to keep them safe.

"Miss Elsie!"

She didn't answer Harry's call. Instead, she concentrated on the man standing with a gun in his hand. "Virgil, I'm not waiting for anyone. I know I put the envelope right here. Please give me a few more minutes to search for it."

He waved the gun in her direction, grabbing her by the upper arm and yanking her in front of him so hard her arm twisted in pain. She let out a yelp.

"Miss Elsie? Where are you? Are you upstairs?" Harry sounded upset.

"Let me answer him. I can tell him to wait for me downstairs," she whispered as fear and a surge of a mother's protectiveness tore through her soul. "I swear to you, Virgil, if you do anything to hurt those children . . ." Her words trailed off. The glint in his eyes sharpened, slicing through her reserve. "Please, let me give you what you want. Let go of my arm so I can open the dresser drawer."

She thought he was going to do just that, and then Harry and Minnie appeared in the doorway of the room. She could see their reflection in her vanity mirror. Harry, seeing the gun pointed at her, dropped the eggs on the floor. They rolled out of the basket, their shells cracking and spilling yolk on the hardwood. Minnie's mouth opened, emitting nothing more than a silent scream.

Chapter Sixteen

Elsie tried to hold back a sob.

Beside her she felt Virgil stiffen as he pressed the gun harder into her side. "Give me those papers! Now!"

Minnie screamed again, only this time Elsie heard her loud and clear. "Don't hurt Miss Elsie! Don't hurt her!"

And then the children were gone from her sight. She called out, "Harry! Minnie!" And hoping they could get to safety, she yelled, "Run! Run and get help!"

Will heard the child's voice and then he heard Elsie yell. He signaled for Lily and John to back him up as he ran across the yard. He'd known the risk he'd taken had been great. After following Virgil here from the homestead, Will had watched him enter the Mitchell's house. His hope that Virgil would find the bonds before Elsie arrived had evaporated like dew on a warm spring day.

Elsie and the children had shown up shortly after him. Staying out of sight had all but killed Will. He watched as Harry and Minnie ran off to chase the chickens and Elsie walked, unsuspecting, into her parents' house. Making sure the children stayed put near the barn, Will had crept closer to the front door of the house. He saw Elsie climb the stairs, taking the same path Virgil had minutes before her.

With his pistol drawn, Will tiptoed into the house. He heard the faint sound of Elsie's voice. Behind him the chickens squawked. Stepping into the shadows of the house, Will waited. And then the unthinkable happened. The children came into the house looking for her. Will raced up the stairs after them. Taking the stairs two at a time, he reached what he assumed was Elsie's bedroom door, gotten Harry's attention, signaled for them to come to him, and pulled them out of harm's way into the hallway. Then he'd motioned for them to hurry back downstairs.

Will's carefully played-out charade was about to come to an end. He stood in the doorway taking in the scene before him. He'd never shot a man, but seeing the woman he loved being held captive brought out something very primal. He knew that if Virgil harmed one hair on Elsie's head, he would shoot.

Virgil shook beside her. Following his slack-jawed gaze, she saw Will. His massive form filled the doorway to her bedroom. He had his gun leveled at Virgil's head.

Clutching Elsie to his chest, Virgil pushed his gun harder against her side.

"I know who you really are, Benton."

Her heart beat faster. *Was Will a part of this scheme of Virgil's? Was that why he'd been stealing away in the middle of the night?* No, she had to be wrong.

"Let her go, Virgil."

"I can't do that. I need those bonds."

"What are you talking about?" Elsie asked. "I don't have any bonds."

"I'm afraid you do. See, that envelope I gave you back in Albany is full of valuable papers."

"Virgil." Her heart ached for him. "What have you become?"

"Nothing more than who I was born to be."

"You need to free her." Will held the gun steady in his hands.

"Will . . . Virgil . . . What is going on here?" Elsie looked away from Will, squirming her body around, trying to get a clearer look at Virgil's face. "Tell me, Virgil, what sort of bonds are in the envelope? You tell me right now!"

"Railroad bonds. It's the only way I can get free of my gambling debts."

"What on earth are you talking about? And what does Will have to do with any of this?"

"Do you want to tell her, lawman, or should I?"

"Lawman?" She swung her gaze to Will. "Will? What's he talking about?"

"Virgil, let her go and then we can sort this mess out. I can make sure you get a good deal from the judge."

"I'm going away for a long time, lawman, and you know it."

"Elsie, you're going to be all right. Everything is going to be all right. I promise. You just have to trust me," Will said.

Finally, she stopped her struggle against Virgil's hold. Looking from one man to the other, she still couldn't believe what she was seeing or hearing. *Will was some sort of lawman? Virgil was a gambler?*

"Are you a sheriff?"

"Oh, he ain't no sheriff, Elsie. He's a bona fide Pinkerton agent. Isn't that right? He's made a life out of slinking around pretending to be someone he's not," Virgil sneered.

"Is he telling the truth?"

Will nodded. "Virgil, I'm not going to ask you again to let Elsie go."

An anger she'd never known existed inside of her exploded. Wrenching her arm out of Virgil's hold, she spun around and yanked open the middle dresser drawer. Rummaging through her underthings, she found the envelope. Yanking it out, she tossed it to Will, who caught it in midair with his free hand. The other still had his gun leveled at Virgil.

"Both of you disgust me." She stomped between them out of the room.

Her knees shook in the aftershock of what had just happened. Pausing at the top of the staircase, she leaned against the wall. Once she was certain she could get down the stairs in one piece, she left the top floor of her parents' house. Behind her Virgil let out a yelp, and then she heard his gun clatter to the floor.

Making her way to the bottom of the stairs, she called out, "Harry! Minnie! Are you in here?" *Where are they?* She ran through the parlor and out onto the porch.

"Harry! Minnie!" she called into the wind, her words echoing around her.

She jumped when she felt a hand on her arm. Turning, she looked into the eyes of none other than John Oliver. He towered above her. She'd forgotten how tall he was. She also noticed that he had a gun in his right hand.

"Mr. Oliver?" Her muddled brain tried to reason why he'd be here. The sun glinted off something on his shirt. She looked away from his eyes and down the length of him, until she found the silver star pinned to his shirt.

"Elsie, are you all right?"

Mr. Oliver was a lawman, too. How could this be? Feeling betrayed all over again, she swallowed hard, forcing down the lump of disbelief in the back of her throat. Her voice came out in a strained whisper. "Where are the children?"

"They are in the barn with—"

She didn't wait for him to finish. She ran from the front porch, through the flock of chickens pecking innocently in the yard. Sending up squawks of protest, they scattered in front of her in different directions. Pushing open the barn door, she raced to where Harry and Minnie were sitting on a hay bale beside a young woman.

It took a minute for her eyes to adjust to the dark interior of the barn. Kneeling before them, she gathered their warm bodies to her. She felt their breath against her neck, felt them hugging her back.

In a coarse voice, she asked, "Are you both all right?"

"Yes, Miss Elsie."

She gasped at the sound of Minnie's voice, remembering now how the dear child had shouted when she found Elsie being held at gunpoint. She could only imagine the fear these children must have felt. She wished they hadn't been a witness to any of this.

"Minnie! You have such a lovely voice." Tears rolled down her cheeks. She hugged her close, never wanting to let her go. Sending up praise and thanksgiving to the Lord above for giving them this miracle.

Eventually Minnie wiggled, bracing her arms against her.

"You're squishing me." Minnie giggled.

Elsie released her but couldn't resist the urge to hold her loosely to her side. "And Harry." Reaching out, she smoothed a lock of hair off his forehead. "You were such a brave young man."

"Is Uncle Will going to capture that bad man?"

"Yes, he is."

A rustling of skirts beside her reminded Elsie that they were not alone in the barn. The woman who'd been caring for the children stood. She gestured for Elsie to take her spot. Elsie sat on the edge of the hay bale next to the children. Slowly, it dawned on her that she'd seen this woman before, only the last time it had been at the saloon, and she had been standing in front of the swinging doors yelling for Will.

Their eyes met. There was no wariness in this woman's eyes, only the same alertness she'd seen in Will's upstairs minutes before.

"Let me guess, you're one of them, too?"

"Yes."

Tilting her head to one side, Elsie pondered this development. "You look different. Your face has changed." She remembered seeing pock-marks and a mole near her nose.

"The saloon girl is one of my disguises."

"Oh." What else could she say?

Sighing, she concentrated on the fact that Minnie's silence had been broken. It almost didn't matter how it had happened. Almost. Elsie's heart began to beat faster as she thought about all the lies and deceit they'd been living with.

"I'm Lily Handland." She extended her hand to Elsie.

Though she preferred not to accept her kindness, Elsie knew how to act politely even in the face of adversity. She shook Miss Handland's hand, surprised to find strength in her grip.

"My name is Elsie Mitchell." It seemed silly to be introducing themselves like they were attending an afternoon tea rather than being involved in the apprehension of a much-sought-after criminal.

Elsie released the woman's hand. Out of the corner of her eye, she saw movement on her parents' front porch. She watched Will bringing Virgil out of the house. Mr. Oliver came out behind them. Even from here she could see the hardness in Will's face. Virgil looked almost relieved to have finally had his burden lifted, though she still had no idea why he'd stolen those railroad bonds. Mr. Oliver came up behind Will and said something to him. Nodding, Will released Virgil, handing him over to Mr. Oliver, who took him to a waiting wagon. In all the excitement, she hadn't even noticed there was an extra one in the yard. Will looked straight ahead at her. She shivered, and then Lily laid a hand on her shoulder.

"Elsie, are you all right? You've been through quite an ordeal. Perhaps I could bring you a cup of water."

She tore her gaze away from Will, fully aware that he was coming to talk to her. Looking at Lily, she replied, "I'm fine."

Will's shadow fell upon her. Elsie wanted to pull the children close to her; she wanted to keep them near where she could touch them, to reassure herself that they were truly unharmed. She didn't know what was going to happen to them now. What would become of the family life they'd worked so hard to build?

Harry ran to Will, throwing himself into his arms. "Uncle Will!" he shouted. Will swung him up into a bear hug.

"Harry." His voice was muffled against Harry's neck.

Elsie blinked back tears.

Minnie sprang from her seat next to Elsie and joined her brother. "Uncle Will. Pick me up, too."

He scooped Minnie up so he was holding a child in each of his strong arms. Elsie felt her world shift.

Will spoke softly: "Minnie, your voice sounds like music to my ears."

Her face beamed. "I thought that terrible man wanted to hurt Miss Elsie. Is he gone now?"

"Yes. He won't be able to hurt anyone ever again."

Setting the children on their feet in front of him, he said to Lily, "Would you mind taking the children back to town?"

"I'd be happy to do so. Shall I wait for you at your house?"

He nodded. Harry and Minnie ran to give Elsie a hug and then left with Lily. Will stood about halfway between her and the door. She thought about fleeing but then realized he probably wouldn't let her leave, so she sat on the hay bale with her hands folded neatly in her lap. The sun's rays slanted through the open doorway. Dust motes danced in the air. Outside, the land looked fresh and clean from the recent storm.

She heard a woodpecker pounding its beak into a nearby tree. She felt Will watching her. Pressing her lips together, she finally lifted her eyes to meet his. From this distance she could only imagine what his thoughts were. Meanwhile, hers were swirling around and around in her mind like a tornado. So many thoughts, and not one of them made any sense.

He broke the silence. "Are you certain you're not hurt?"

"I'm fine."

Walking through the sun's rays, he came to where she sat. She noticed the mud caked to his boots and staining the lower portion of his black pants. His long duster coat rested loosely over his muscular frame. She looked at the lips that had kissed her. The hands that had held her face. She sighed, closing her eyes, blocking out his image.

Kneeling in front of her, he made an attempt to take her hands in his. She curled them into fists in her lap.

He dropped his hands to his thighs. "Elsie," he spoke her name so softly she had to strain to hear it.

He tucked a hand under her chin, lifting her face, forcing her to look into his eyes. She fought the urge to cry. She would not cry now.

"I'd like to go home." The words came out before she realized she was referring to their home in town. And now that would all change. The place was never her home. The past months had been nothing more than a ruse. Will had used her for his subterfuge. John Oliver had knowingly played a part in the deceit. The only ones who remained innocent were the only ones who mattered. Harry and Minnie.

Whatever had been growing between Will and her had never really existed. She didn't want to believe that all they'd shared, all they'd built, had been nothing more than some part of a scheme set in motion the minute she'd met him at the train station in Albany. And even before that—from the time Virgil had spotted her in that restaurant, begging her to let him come see her. She'd taken his package, offering up her forgiveness to him. She'd been nothing more than a fool. Not once, but twice. Her stomach twisted in knots. Sorrow filled her.

Will leaned in, resting his forehead against hers.

"I never intended for any of this to happen."

His breath warmed her cold cheeks. "I'm sure you didn't." Her lips trembled. "Oh . . . Will . . . How could you lie to me?"

"Elsie, I'm sorry." Wrapping his arms around her, he tried to pull her against his solid chest.

She pushed against him. "Don't."

He released her. Rising slowly, he said, "This is who I am. I am an agent with the Pinkertons. I've been with the organization for over five years now."

"All those late nights when you told me you were working at the lumber camp, where were you?"

"Tracking the bond thief."

"Virgil?"

He nodded. "Only I didn't know it was him. We had no idea who we were looking for until yesterday, and then all the pieces fell into place."

"I don't understand how you could profess to love those children and yet you had no problem putting them in such grave danger. How could you do that?" Her heart ached for them. "How could you put me in danger? Until today I had no idea the kind of man Virgil had become. But you suspected him all along, didn't you?"

She watched him set his mouth in a grim line, swallow, and take in a deep breath. She wondered what lie he was fixing to tell her now. She stood.

"I had to be positive Virgil Jensen was the man we'd been hunting. I didn't want him coming around you. But I had no choice."

Folding her arms across her chest, she replied, "You could have told me the truth."

He stepped in front of her so they stood toe to toe. "And you could have ended up dead if I had." He raked a hand through his hair.

Poking him in the chest, she said, "Maybe I could have helped you. And then *this* might not have happened." She waved a hand through the air in frustration.

"Elsie, how can I make you understand how dangerous my job is? You can't just *help* me."

Not knowing what else to do, she shook her head and turned away from him.

She heard him blow out a breath, and then he said in a voice filled with resignation, "We should head back to town."

"Lily took the wagon."

"I have a mount here."

Walking out into the sunshine, she said, "I'd rather walk, thank you."

"Elsie, don't be so stubborn. You take the mount, and I'll walk beside you."

Straightening her spine, she pushed him aside and strode past the horse, following the pathway that led to town. She knew the way by heart. Every twist and turn along the way. The walk would do her good, give her time to get control of the anger brewing inside her. She stepped into a puddle, the soft earth giving way beneath her feet, sending squishy, muddy water over her shoes.

Yanking her skirts higher to save them from further ruin, she let out a frustrated yelp. Behind her she heard Will growl.

"Elsie, get on the horse," he ordered.

Fervently she shook her head, stomping onward.

"Woman!" he roared.

She stood stock-still.

His voice softened. "Please, get on the horse."

Turning around, she found herself staring up at both him and the horse. Will rested an elbow on the saddle, leaning in, leveling a steely gaze at her. She weighed her options. She could continue to be stubborn and walk through the ruts and dodge the mud puddles all the way to town, thereby ruining a perfectly good dress, or she could get on the horse and save what she had left of her pride.

Setting her jaw, she asked, "I assume you'll be dismounting?"

Doing just that, he helped her up into the saddle. She hadn't been on a horse in years, and because this wasn't a sidesaddle, she had to sit astride with her skirts bunched up and showing off her calves. But she soon discovered that was the least of her worries because Will quickly remounted the horse to sit right behind her. She let out a gasp as his body settled against hers.

"Elsie, I've had a long twenty-four hours and I'm not going to be a gentleman and let you have this horse all to yourself. There are things I need to tend to in a timely manner."

His arms stretched around her as he gathered the reins in his hands. He nudged the horse into a quick gait. Elsie hung on for dear life. The movement sent her back against Will's chest. She squirmed, trying to find a comfortable position on the hard leather.

"Settle down or you're going to spook the horse."

"You could just set me back on the ground."

"I could, but I'm not going to." His chin touched the top of her head.

Being this close to him soon proved to be unbearable. "Please, Will," she begged him, "put me down."

Chapter Seventeen

"I can't let you go." Will couldn't give in to her request. And knowing how much pain he caused her today made holding on to her that much more important. He thought that if he let Elsie down, she would run from him without ever looking back. And he wouldn't blame her if she wanted to do that. He couldn't bear the thought of her leaving him.

Her being in harm's way this afternoon had been all his doing.

In front of him Elsie shifted her weight. Fighting the urge to pull her closer, he adjusted his body in the saddle so she would have a bit more room. Except moving against her made him want to kiss her again and again just to prove that she really was safe in his arms.

Not one to question his deeds, Will wondered if he could have done anything differently. Over and over the scene played out in his mind. Virgil holding Elsie to his side with a gun against her rib cage. Then the look in her eyes . . . She'd been angry and frightened. Though he suspected her fear wasn't for herself. No, she had put Harry's and Minnie's well-being before her own like she'd done every day from the time they'd first met.

Helping her at the train station in Albany. Then her agreeing to take the job of live-in caregiver for complete strangers. All the little things she'd set about doing to make the old Oliver house a home. Caring for and loving the children like they were her own flesh and blood. Hadn't she been the one to make sure they'd said their prayers and attended church every Sunday? Elsie had shared her faith and trust in the Lord with such pride and conviction.

And in one moment of clarity, Will knew Elsie had given him all the things she'd so freely given to the children. And what had he done? Handed all those things back to her, and on more than one occasion, even going so far as to scoff at her faith in something unseen.

She'd had faith in their relationship, enduring his absences at the dinner table and in the church pew. He remembered the kisses they'd shared. He knew she felt the same way he did, that there could be something more between them.

Sighing against her, Will knew he'd gone too far with his subterfuge. She would never forgive him for making their life a lie.

They rounded the last corner in the road. Up ahead the little town of Heartston, New York, lay at the foot of the great Adirondack High Peaks. The leaves on the trees glistened in the warm sunlight. As they grew close, he heard voices chattering excitedly.

"Will, put me down right now."

Elsie did her best to squirm out of his hold by jabbing her elbow into his ribs. He sucked in a quick breath of pain. She was stronger than she looked.

"I told you, I don't want you walking when there's a perfectly good horse for you to ride."

Craning her neck to look up at him, he met her turbulent gaze. He saw the raw panic on her face and the stark fear in her widened eyes.

"Don't you understand? Please, Will, I can't let anyone see me like this." She let out a sob.

He felt an ache growing deep in his chest because he did understand. Being a proud young woman, he knew it would be hard for her to let anyone see her in such a fragile state. He tugged on the reins, pulling the horse to a stop at the edge of the village. Dismounting, he reached up, putting his hands around her waist. She pressed her hands against his shoulders as he gently lifted her to the ground.

Wrapping his arms around her trembling form, he stroked her back, hoping to give her some comfort. Immediately, she stiffened beneath his touch. Straightening her spine, she struggled to push his arms aside. He held firm.

"Elsie, don't leave me like this." He knew his words were born of hopelessness, of his selfish need to make her stay by his side.

Wrenching her body away from his, she shook her head, the force of the movement sending strands of her dark hair flying about her face and shoulders. He started to reach out to catch those silken locks between his fingers. Her fierce look stopped his movement.

He let her go. Standing in the brilliant sunshine, with the birds chattering merrily around him, he let the only woman he ever loved walk away. A hollow feeling settled deep inside him, working its way into his heart. Leading the horse, he walked the rest of the way to the village.

Pausing at the edge of the yard, Elsie took a moment to pull herself together. She ran a hand through her hair, trying to neaten the mess. She pressed her hands down the front of her dress, trying to smooth out the wrinkles. She frowned at the dried mud staining the hem of her dress, caked to the heels and toes of her shoes. Her clothes were in ruins. She forced herself to hold back her sobs. It wouldn't do for the children to find her like this.

Using the backs of her hands, she wiped her eyes dry. She made her way to the front porch. She could hear the sound of the children's voices coming from inside the house. Pausing just for a minute longer on the bottom step, she took in the sweet sound of Minnie's voice. She didn't think she'd ever grow tired of hearing her.

She opened the front door. There they were in the parlor, sitting on the settee, looking through one of their favorite storybooks. Their faces looked freshly scrubbed.

"Miss Mitchell! I'm so glad you're home." Lily Handland came out of the kitchen with a dish towel in her hand. "I've just finished making a snack for the children."

She peered at Elsie. Taking in her tear-stained face, she said, "You look like you could use a good warm bath."

Sucking her upper lip between her teeth, Elsie did her best to keep her emotions at bay. She simply would not fall apart in front of the twins. Though they looked peaceful and serene right now, she suspected that later, after Lily had gone and they were left alone, things might take a turn.

The screen door creaked on its hinges. Turning around, she'd never been so thankful to see her mother.

"Oh!" Rushing into the welcoming arms, she wept.

"I'll take the children outside." Lily moved by them.

From over her mother's shoulder, Elsie caught sight of Harry's concerned face. She attempted to smile at him, but she was sure it came off looking more like a grimace.

"Elsie. My poor dear. There. There." Her mother patted her lovingly on the back. Ushering her into the kitchen, she helped her sit at the table.

She watched her mother take the simmering kettle off the back burner and pour the steamy water into the basin sitting alongside the sink. Then she pumped a bit of cold water into it. Finding a clean cloth, she dipped it in the warm water and placed it in Elsie's hands. When Elsie sat there unmoving, her mother picked up the cloth and began to gently wipe her face.

"The town is bustling with activity."

Laying a hand over her mother's, she stopped her from continuing the ministrations. "Mama, you can tell me what's being said."

Pulling a chair beside hers, her mother sat down. "They're saying that Virgil is a criminal. Is this true?"

"Yes."

"And somehow Will is a part of all this."

"He's an agent for the Pinkertons."

"Who are they?"

"They're a detective agency."

She nodded, although Elsie knew her mother had no idea who Will worked for. It really didn't matter. Suddenly she felt bone-weary, as if she could lie in her bed and sleep for days. But she couldn't do that. There was so much left to settle.

"I'm worried about the children."

Patting her on the arm, her mother said, "You know how resilient children can be."

"Minnie is speaking." Elsie's heart lifted a bit with the knowledge that at least one thing had gone right today.

"That's wonderful news! We should send up prayers of thanksgiving."

"Oh, Mama, what have I done?" She pressed her hand against her mouth to still the fresh sobs. "I thought I'd been doing what the Lord intended for me to do. I accepted the offer of this job to help save money to pay for my future travels. I knew I could be of service to his little family. But then . . ." She hesitated.

Her mother tucked a hand under her chin, tipping her head so she could see into her eyes, a gesture that brought to mind Elsie's childhood days. It calmed her. Her mother's brown eyes looked at her, steady and calm, when all Elsie could see in front of her was the storm swirling around them.

"But then you fell in love with William Benton." Her mother finished her thoughts.

Blinking back tears, Elsie nodded. "Yes, I did. I didn't want or expect this to happen."

Dropping her hand, her mother said, "Sometimes the Lord has bigger plans."

"And he never gives us more than we can handle. But I'm afraid that Will went too far by putting us in danger."

Elsie couldn't believe she had let herself be taken in by another man who'd betrayed her and used her to further his gains. "Mama, I'm not sure I can forgive him."

"You forgave Virgil, and you will forgive your gentleman."

"Be that as it may, I regret forgiving Virgil. His intentions toward me were never good, you know. As for Will, let's just say I may have learned my lesson concerning men the hard way."

"Elsie, it's not like you to be so bitter."

"I've had a long day, Mama. Perhaps I will lie down for a bit." Rising, she added, "But first I need to check on the children."

Accompanying her to the front porch, her mother said, "They seem to be happy enough on those swings. Look at how high they're going."

The swings that Will had put up. She tried not to think of all the other things they'd done to make this a better place for the children. The hurt of his betrayal was too fresh.

Lily saw Elsie and her mother standing in the doorway, so leaving the children to play, she joined them.

"Elsie, Will sent over a message that there will be dinner for everyone at the restaurant. After what happened today, he doesn't want to burden you with any chores."

"That's mighty nice of him, considering we wouldn't be in this predicament if it hadn't been for his actions."

Lily fixed a sharpened gaze on her. "Mrs. Mitchell, would you mind watching the children while I have a word with your daughter?"

"Go on, Mama. I'll be fine."

Lily didn't waste any time getting to the point of her conversation. "I've known William Benton for a long time. We've worked together on many cases for the Pinkerton Detective Agency. If I know one thing about him, it's that he's the most loyal person I know. And he doesn't give his affections easily."

Walking out onto the porch, Elsie sat in one of the rockers, yet another reminder of Will. "I know he's loyal. Otherwise, he wouldn't have kept his job a secret from me."

"He wants to do what's right."

Elsie couldn't bear to hear Lily sing any more praises for Will. She needed some time alone to think. She thought it a good idea that the children join their uncle for dinner. He could see for himself that they were doing all right. No doubt, they needed to see him, too.

"Take the children to meet their uncle. Please give Will my regrets. As much as a dinner out would be tempting, I'm afraid I'm not up to being out in public just yet." She knew her words came out sounding wooden.

The last part of her statement held the truth. She didn't think she could abide by all the stares and well-meaning concerns of her neighbors and friends. She felt certain that word of what had happened at her parents' house had spread like a wildfire throughout the small town.

"I will do as you ask, but not before I say one more thing. Will is in love with you. He's not going to let you go easily, Elsie. Think on that while we're gone." In a swirl of skirts the woman turned and went down the front steps.

Her mother came back onto the porch, and Elsie told her to have her father bring the wagon by in an hour's time. When her mother started to protest, Elsie hugged her, and then releasing her, she sent her off.

Elsie heard Lily telling the children they'd be going to meet their uncle. Harry turned to look at her, seeking her permission. She raised her hand, forcing a smile to her face, and waved them off.

She sat on the porch for a long time after they were gone, thinking about the day's events, working at putting all the pieces together. She couldn't imagine what had led to Virgil's downfall.

She'd known of him for a long time before they'd started seeing each other. When he'd come courting, he seemed like a fine gentleman, and she, being well on her way to spinsterhood, had been flattered by his attentions. He'd proposed marriage one day and she'd accepted, and then he broke their engagement off. Leaving her alone. She'd no idea he'd been gambling away money as fast as it came to him.

And then there was the matter of Will. Elsie didn't want to think about what might have been. The pain in her heart was still so fresh, like a raw, open wound.

Tipping her head back, she watched a robin tend to babies in a nest in the eave of the porch. She'd been tending to Harry and Minnie like they were her babies . . . only they didn't belong to her. Folding her hands in her lap, she bowed her head. The prayer she sent forth held anguish and desperation. She prayed for the strength to go on without the children, without Will. She prayed that she'd be able to find it in her heart to one day stop loving the man. Ending with an amen, she got up from the rocker and made her way to her quarters.

Finding her traveling satchel, she began stuffing her dresses and toiletries inside. When she'd fit as much as the container would hold, she latched it closed. She would send her father back for the remainder of her belongings. She needed to be gone before Will and the children came home. With shaking hands, she went into the kitchen. It took her a minute to find a writing utensil and some paper. Quickly she scribbled a note to Will, hoping he would understand her actions and know this was the right thing for her to do.

Gathering her schoolwork, and taking her shawl off the coatrack, she picked up the handle of the satchel and walked out the front door, slamming up against the wall of Will's chest.

"*Oof!*" She exhaled sharply. "What are you doing here?" she snapped.

Chapter Eighteen

"I came to check on you."

Stepping to one side, she tried to look around him to see if the children were with him, but in shifting his stance to mirror her movement, he blocked her.

"Mr. Benton!" she huffed out in exasperation. "Are Harry and Minnie with you? Because I don't want them to see me leaving."

"They're enjoying supper with Lily."

"Lily! She must have overheard me telling my mother to have my father bring the wagon around for me. So she told you I'd be leaving?"

"She did."

When he didn't say anything more, Elsie thought he might let her go without a fight, but she'd never been more wrong.

Edging closer to her, he said, "You can't leave."

"Don't you see? I can't stay here anymore."

He countered, "We can work this out."

Shaking her head, she tried to push past him, but he appeared to be as unmovable as the mountains off in the distance. She leaned an elbow into his side, pushing against him. "Please. Let me leave before Harry and Minnie come home."

He brought his arms down, laying his hands along her upper arms. She felt his strength and the warmth from his fingertips penetrating the sleeves of her dress. She smelled his scent, masculine and woodsy. His chambray shirt moved against his chest as he took in a breath. Exhaling, he rested his chin lightly atop her head.

"Stay."

She shook her head. She wanted to hear him say that he loved her. She wanted him to admit he'd been wrong to not tell her who he really was.

"No."

"Please."

Her father's wagon rattled to a stop at the end of the walkway. Will released his hold on her.

"No." She firmly repeated the word even though every fiber of her being shouted for her to stay.

Lowering her head so she wouldn't have to see her pain reflected in his eyes, she scurried down the walkway. But not before she heard the sound of Minnie's voice off in the distance. The sound brought such joy and sorrow to her heart at the same time.

Will had come up behind her. "Don't leave them, Elsie."

Dropping her bag to the walkway, she turned on him. "How dare you use those children to further your gain? Haven't you done that enough already?"

"I can understand how you might see things that way, Elsie. But I did not use them."

"But you did, Will. You brought them here, letting them believe you would be taking care of them, letting them think that this was going to be their home. When the only reason you came here to begin with was because you were chasing down your bond thief."

Swiping the tears from her cheeks, she continued, "What kind of man uses children in such a manner?"

"That was never my intent. Deep in your heart you know it. Harry and Minnie are my flesh and blood. I would never do anything to hurt them."

"And what about me, Will? What about us? I know you've been aware of the feelings growing between us." Tilting her head at him, she said, "And yet you chose to lie to me at every turn. I can't forget about that. And I can't trust that you'll ever be honest with me. I can't forgive you."

"I hear the children coming. Elsie, please, think about what you're leaving will do."

Honestly, she wanted to throttle the man. But he was right. Harry and Minnie didn't deserve to be the ones hurt by their actions. They were the true innocents in this mess. Placing her hands on her hips, she squared her shoulders.

"I'll stay. But make no mistake about my decision, Mr. Benton. I'm doing this for that little boy and girl. No one else except them."

It wasn't lost on Will that Elsie had taken to calling him Mr. Benton again. Still, he wanted to shout from the mountaintop with jubilation. Tamping down his feeling of relief and, yes, even joy, Will knew he had a long way to go to earn her forgiveness. Convincing her to stay was a good start. He watched her go over to speak to her father. He kissed his daughter on the forehead and then gave Will a stern look.

The man hadn't cared much for Will before all this had happened. He imagined Mr. Mitchell really didn't wish his daughter to be living here now. Picking up Elsie's bag, he headed on into the house. After leaving her things in her quarters, he came back into the kitchen, noticing the note she'd left propped up against the flowers in the center of the table. Picking up the piece of paper, he read what she'd written. The words were slanted on the page in her elegant handwriting.

Mr. Benton,

I'm afraid I cannot abide by your recent actions. I feel that my services are no longer needed in your home. I will be returning to my parents' house. Please know that Harry and Minnie are welcome to come visit me anytime they wish. I will keep you all in my prayers.

Sincerely,
Elsie Mitchell

He frowned, realizing his victory at convincing her to stay was only a small step in the long process of gaining her trust and affections again. He heard the front door open and close. The floorboards in the parlor creaked as her heels tapped lightly over it.

She entered the kitchen with her mouth drawn in a thin line. Her eyes narrowed when she saw that he held her good-bye note in his hand. In two short steps she came to the table, snatching the paper from him.

"I guess we won't be needing this." Crumpling the paper into a ball, she tossed it in the waste bin.

"Elsie—" He reached out to her.

She batted his hand away. "I think you should address me as Miss Mitchell."

Giving a shake of his head, he said, "No. I'll be calling you Elsie."

"Suit yourself. I'm going to unpack my bag. Then I think I'll take a rest before the children come home."

"But what about your supper? Aren't you hungry?"

"I'm afraid I don't have much of an appetite. It's been a long day, and tomorrow is the start of another school week."

He certainly had tossed her life upside down. There was no avoiding that, and he well knew it. Still, he wouldn't have changed a thing about the way he'd handled this case. At the time he'd met her, his first loyalty had been to his job. He didn't imagine she'd like to hear that.

He'd done his job. Maybe not in the way she would have liked, but he'd caught the bond thief just like he'd set out to do.

"I'll be out on the porch should you need anything."

"Fine." Turning away from him, she went into her rooms. The door shut firmly behind her.

Will wasn't sure, but he could have sworn he heard her latch the lock on the door. She was angrier than he'd ever seen. He guessed he'd just have to wait her out, then they could talk this through. Except that was going to be easier said than done.

The children arrived home shortly afterward. Not wanting to disturb Elsie, he helped them get ready for bed.

"Is Miss Elsie feeling sickly?" Harry asked as Will helped him into his nightclothes.

"No. She's had a very long day."

"I was so afraid when we found her with that man. He had a gun. Did you hear Minnie scream? She was really loud." Harry grinned.

"Yes, she was." Will ruffled the little girl's hair.

"I thought that terrible man was going to hurt our Miss Elsie. I'm glad you were there, Uncle Will."

Uncle Will. He didn't think he'd ever get tired of hearing her say his name. "Well, I can't tell you how happy everyone is that you're speaking again, Minnie."

Hugging Hazel, she said, "I had to yell. How else would you have known where to find us?"

"But you didn't know I was out in the yard."

"No. But I prayed real hard, and the Lord heard me and he sent you and Miss Lily to find us."

Will didn't know what to say to that, so he just finished getting them ready for bed. Once they were safely tucked in with the yellow patchwork quilt covering them up to their chins, he bent to give them each a kiss on the forehead.

Harry reminded him, "Uncle Will, we still need to say our prayers."

Two sets of hands popped out from underneath the blankets. Both children folded their hands neatly under their chins.

Minnie exclaimed, "I'm going to say our prayers tonight, Harry! You don't always get them right."

"You could have told me what you wanted me to say."

Giggling, Minnie began, "Dear Lord, thank you for sending Uncle Will to save us. Thank you for sending Miss Lily, too. She's very nice. Specially, thank you for watching over Miss Elsie and Uncle Will. Amen."

She settled back against her pillow and then quickly shot back up to a sitting position. Folding her hands once more, she added, "I almost forgot. Please make Uncle Will and Miss Elsie smile again. Amen."

For a few minutes Will couldn't move. And then, clearing his throat, he stood. "You two have a good night's sleep. I'll see you in the morning."

"Don't forget to leave the lamp on low like Miss Elsie always does," Harry reminded him.

Making his way down the staircase, he wondered what Elsie would think if she'd heard Minnie's last prayer. No doubt she'd make a run for the hills. But the girl's prayerful request got him to pondering what life could be like if he and Elsie were to marry. He could settle here full-time. Hearing Minnie's voice had changed him on the inside. Being here in this house . . . no, this home . . . made him realize how good it felt to be in the same bed every night. Except his life had changed in more ways than just having the same bed to come home to every night.

He came home to people who loved him and needed him. Will hadn't been needed by anyone in a long time. He needed them, too.

He didn't want to go back out on the road, chasing down the next criminal, closing the next case. He wanted to be here with Harry and Minnie. And Elsie.

He heard a pot rattle on the stove. Entering the kitchen, he saw her standing there with her hair loose, the ends hanging down, brushing against the curve of her waist. She'd changed out of her mud-stained dress into her nightclothes. Her cream-colored wrapper was tied snuggly about her.

She turned around when she heard him enter the kitchen. Her face had been scrubbed clean and now looked pale in the glow of the lantern light. But her violet eyes were wide and staring right at him. She looked beautiful. He wanted to say those words to her. But he didn't think in her state of anger she'd be happy to hear them. She opened her mouth as if to speak and then quickly snapped it shut. She nibbled on her bottom lip. He saw her toe tapping beneath the hem of her nightgown. He bit back a grin. To him, this marked some progress in their standoff. It meant she was ready for a fight. Well, so was he.

"I've been thinking about our circumstances."

Leaning against the doorjamb, he carefully folded his arms across his chest. "Have you now."

"Yes. I've decided some new rules need to be in place."

"More rules. Haven't I been abiding by them enough already?"

She tipped her chin down, leveling her gaze on him. "Hardly."

"Fine. Go on."

"We will carry on civil conversations for the sake of the children, but nothing more. Dinner will be on the table at six o'clock and you *will* be present."

"I'll be here for dinner."

As soon as the water heated to boiling, Elsie concentrated on making a pot of tea. While she did that, Will moved about the kitchen, finding a plate of day-old cookies. He put them on the table in front of her.

"Thank you," she whispered.

He realized her bravado had dwindled away and there were tears in her eyes. Pulling out the chair next to her, he placed one hand over hers.

"Hey. I know what happened today was frightening."

He felt her fingers stiffen beneath his, but she didn't pull away.

"I didn't expect Virgil to go crazy." Her chin quivered. "I didn't expect to learn that you are not the man I thought you were. I'm not sure I can just forget about your deceptions. It's like there's this part of you that I never knew about."

He bowed his head, feeling grief-stricken. Bringing her hand to his lips, he kissed her fingertips. The ache inside of him was so great he didn't know what to do with it all. He knew what Elsie would say if he told her about his pain. She'd tell him to bring his worries to the Lord. He sighed. He wasn't ready to do that, either.

Still holding firmly to her hand, he rested his elbows on the table-top. "Believe me when I tell you, I never, ever meant for you to get hurt."

"I know."

"Let me make this up to you, Elsie."

He felt her try to work her hand free, and he gently tightened his hold, pulling her to him. Doing the one thing he'd wanted to do since he'd rescued her, he used his free hand to caress her face. Her skin reminded him again of the day they'd met at the train station in Albany, of how he'd picked her stockings up off the rough platform. Those stockings had felt so silky and soft as they threaded through his fingers, slipping into her hands. Now her skin felt silky and soft to his touch. Yet he could feel Elsie slipping away from him. He refused to let her go so easily.

Moving his hand to her chin, he urged her toward him until their lips touched.

Chapter Nineteen

Pushing her hands against the hardness of his chest, she let out a frustrated yelp. "Mr. Benton! You cannot just kiss our problems away."

"Why not?" he asked.

"Because I said so." Pushing away from him and the table, she left her tea and stale cookies and went back to her bedroom.

The next day she got up and went about the usual morning routine, which involved breakfast, filling everyone's lunch boxes, and heading off to the schoolhouse. Except she spoke only to the children. Leaning against the sink, Will watched out the window as the trio made their way down to the village. He could see Minnie's mouth moving and Elsie smiling at whatever the little girl said.

Moving away from the window, he set about his day. His first order of business would be seeing to the transfer of Virgil Jensen. Virgil would be leaving on the next train bound for Albany. Since he'd already confessed to his crimes, Virgil would be sentenced and placed in a federal prison. All Will needed to do was sign off on some paperwork and hand him over.

A knock sounded at the front door. He opened it to find Lily Handland standing there, looking as fresh as a daisy. Her blonde hair was pulled back in a bun at the nape of her neck. Her blue eyes danced with mischief. Batting her long lashes at him, she smiled.

"Good morning, Lily."

"Good morning, Will. I just passed Elsie and the children heading for school. How did things go last night?"

Grabbing his hat off the hook on the wall, he replied, "As well as can be expected." He joined her on the porch.

"I see."

"Has Virgil signed his confession?"

Accompanying him down the path, she nodded. "He's all ready for the transfer." In the next breath, she said, "Elsie seems like a fine woman."

"Don't go there, Lily."

"Why not?"

He slanted a glance at her. "Because I said so."

"You could make it work with her, you know."

"I know."

They came to a stop at the town jail. "Well, let me know if you need my help."

"Thanks, I'll be fine." He'd already been thinking about how he could get back in Elsie's good graces. Today would be the start of a new beginning with her, and he didn't care that she was barely speaking to him.

Elsie spent a good portion of the school day working with the children on the travel project. The older students had each picked a place they'd like to travel to and had been gathering information about those locations. The younger students were beginning to learn about history, and

Elsie had let them look at the pictures in her travel guide so they could see what lay beyond Heartston. They wanted to know where she'd been. So she told them about traveling by train down to Albany and how she ate oysters and fish from the Hudson River.

One of her older students asked her where she hoped to travel to next, reminding her of how she'd wanted to travel abroad on an ocean liner. Those dreams of adventure seemed like they came from a lifetime ago. Long before she'd met William Benton and his family. How her life had changed over the past few months. Those ambitions now seemed so inconsequential, so trite and so very selfish. Maybe one day she would get there, but for now she would immerse herself in the classroom project.

The week went by, and she fell into a routine, getting up each day to find Will in the kitchen starting breakfast. Every night as promised he returned from his day to be at the dinner table at precisely six o'clock. She didn't ask where he'd been. On Friday, Will informed her that he would be leaving work early to pick up the children from school. Even if she thought it an odd gesture, she decided not to question his motives. Several times during the week she caught Will and the children with their heads together, whispering.

It was good for them to be spending time together, especially if he decided he'd no longer be needing her services. She realized she had to prepare for that possibility. In low spirits she closed up the school for the weekend and turned to find Amy waiting for her in the school yard.

"Isn't this a lovely surprise?" She embraced her friend. Pulling back, she noticed that Amy looked to be happy about something.

"I had a telegram from my mother this afternoon. They will be arriving next Sunday!"

"You must be so relieved."

"Oh, I am! Not that I've minded running the bakery in their absence, but land's sakes I'm tired of getting up before the crack of dawn every morning."

Amy wandered past Elsie, taking a seat on the steps. Patting the spot next to her, she invited Elsie to join her. "Come sit with me for a few minutes."

"I should be getting back to the house." Elsie knew she'd been keeping to herself. She'd been avoiding going into town like the plague. No doubt everyone had been babbling away about Virgil and how he'd held her at gunpoint.

"I've been so worried about you. Everyone has."

"I'm sorry I haven't stopped in to visit you. I just can't bear to come to town." She walked the few short paces back to the staircase.

"I heard Virgil has been taken back to Albany," Amy said.

Elsie nodded, sitting next to her. "Yes. Will put him on the train on Monday afternoon. I wanted to go and say my piece to Virgil, but I just couldn't bring myself to do so."

"Elsie, the man had already put you through enough. You did the right thing by staying away."

"I suppose. Maybe one day I'll send him a letter."

"Why would you do that?"

Shielding her eyes against the sun, she turned to look at her friend. "I don't like leaving things open-ended."

"You forgave him before."

"I tried, and after last week I wished I hadn't. Virgil has a troubled soul. Perhaps the time in prison will reform him."

Elsie looked through the dappled sunlight toward the village. She'd missed her normal routine. Harry and Minnie loved stopping by the bakery on their way home, and she hadn't been able to bring herself to walk the short distance for fear she'd be stopped by a well-meaning neighbor or, worse yet, Mr. Moore. The owner of the dry-goods store kept close tabs on the goings-on here in Heartston. She felt certain her escapade had kept him busy. She didn't think she could abide by any of her neighbors' sympathies even if they were well-intentioned.

Amy placed her hand over Elsie's, saying, "I feel terrible about everything that happened to you. You have to know there have been a lot of prayers of thanksgiving said on your behalf."

A sudden onslaught of tears took Elsie by surprise. She'd thought she was all cried out. "That's nice to know."

Swallowing, she blew out an unsteady breath. Then, gathering her strength, she said, "Will has become very attentive. He's been home every night on time for dinner. And he helps the children with their schoolwork. It's a wonderful sight to see him working with Harry as he deciphers the arithmetic problems he's been trying so hard to master. And Minnie reads aloud to Will every night."

"Elsie, I can see the love you have for them. And I'm not just talking about the children. Any fool can tell just by looking at the way you light up when you mention Will's name that you love that man."

She glanced down at her hands. "I've been trying hard not to love him."

Beside her, Amy chuckled. "Perhaps what I'm about to tell you will persuade you. He donated a large sum of money to the church."

She gasped in disbelief. "How do you know this?"

"The pastor's wife mentioned it at the last Lord's Acre Picnic meeting."

Elsie had been so wrapped up in her own problems that she'd completely forgotten about the meeting. "Oh my, the meeting slipped my mind."

"No one expected you to be there. Besides, you know that the pastor's wife may let us think we're doing things to help when really she runs the show." Amy laughed.

"That's this Sunday. The children will be attending their first one."

Laying a hand on her arm, Amy brought Elsie's attention back to Will. "Will gave the church a lot of money, Elsie. Enough to make some repairs to the building and buy those new hymnals."

"That's very generous of him."

"I think he did it to impress you."

"I don't need to be impressed."

"You need to make peace with all that happened."

Nodding, she knew Amy was right. "I'm trying. Truly I am."

Amy stood, shaking her skirts out. Stepping onto the dirt, she turned to look down at Elsie. Determination etched her face; care and love filled her eyes. "Elsie, I feel in my heart that William Benton is a good man. I think he loves you. True love doesn't come along very often. Remember that."

Standing, Elsie hugged her. "Thank you."

"I'll see you first thing Sunday morning. The pastor's wife said she's arranged for the tables to be set up out in the churchyard tomorrow, so all we'll need to do is cover them with cloths when we get there."

"I'll see you then." She watched Amy walk to the edge of the school yard, then yelled, "Amy, wait." Rushing to her, she linked her arm through her friend's. "I think I'll walk home through town today."

As it turned out, even those who tipped their hats to her in greeting or said hello to her as they passed by made no mention of what had transpired. There were no stares of recrimination like she'd expected. Elsie felt silly for worrying over nothing. Coming into the walkway leading to the house, she was surprised to find that Minnie and Harry were not outside enjoying the remains of another gorgeous afternoon.

The silence alarmed her. Rushing up onto the porch, she entered the house out of breath from the exertion. The parlor was empty, too. "Will?" she called out, trying to keep the panic out of her voice.

"We're in the kitchen," he answered.

Laying a hand over her heart in relief, she practically ran the last steps to the room. She pulled up short at the sight that greeted her. The kitchen had been transformed. The table had a new flowered cloth covering it. On top of that were four place settings of the finest china Elsie had ever seen. Upon closer inspection, she realized the pattern looked similar to the ones she'd seen adorning the dining tables depicted in the pages of her travel book.

In addition to this, silver place settings and white cloth napkins flanked the dishes. Tall drinking glasses were filled with water. The center of the table held a tall glass vase filled with lovely daisies, Queen Anne's lace, and shoots of purple lavender.

"Will!" She breathed out his name. "The table looks lovely!"

"Harry and I picked the flowers for you, Miss Elsie," Minnie informed her.

Harry and Minnie, each wearing their Sunday-best outfits, stood at their seats.

"They're beautiful!" She clapped her hands together in delight, feeling pride swelling from their smiles. Will hadn't moved from his position in front of the stove. And then she noticed the savory scent wafting from a pot bubbling on the back burner. Bringing her gaze back to him, she tipped her head to one side, realizing he looked different.

"You look nice all clean-shaven, and your hair . . ."

"Is much shorter," he finished, brushing his hand over the top of his head. "I decided it was high time I visited the barber shop. I had him shave off my beard, too." He rubbed his hand along his smooth jaw.

He looked so handsome standing there in his freshly laundered white shirt and black pants. His face looked different, too. Gone were the lines of worry that had bracketed his eyes and mouth for as long as she'd known him. Glancing down at the children, she thought they all looked wonderful. Elsie didn't know what she'd done to deserve this treat. Her heart swelled with love.

"Harry, you can show Miss Elsie to her seat now."

Walking around the back of the table, Harry took hold of her hand and led her to her seat at one end of the table. She allowed him to pull out the chair for her.

"My, you are growing up to be quite the gentleman. Thank you, Harry."

Minnie followed close behind them, and taking the cloth napkin from Elsie's place setting, she shook the bit of fabric out and laid it across Elsie's lap.

Elsie drew the little girl close to her side, dropping a kiss on top of her head. "Thank you, Minnie. You did a proper job with the napkin."

She wondered how long they'd been rehearsing this. Raising her eyes, she found Will watching them. Elsie gave him a brilliant smile, mouthing a thank-you to him. He gave her a slight bow from the waist. Elsie actually found herself giggling like a schoolgirl.

"Harry and Minnie, you can sit at the table, too. I'll bring the stew over," Will instructed.

While the children settled themselves, he took a pot holder from the hook on the wall. Lifting the black kettle's handle, he brought the wonderfully scented meal to the table. He took Elsie's plate first, dishing out a succulent beef stew with thick, gravy-coated chunks of carrots and potatoes and bite-sized pieces of meat.

"Will, had I known you could cook like this, I would have had you helping out with more of the meals," she said, teasing him.

Harry and Minnie both giggled.

Will actually looked a bit chagrined. "I'm afraid I must confess I didn't cook this. I purchased the dinner from the restaurant in town."

It didn't matter to her who prepared the meal. What mattered most to her was that Will had gone to a great deal of effort on her behalf. Elsie couldn't remember the last time anyone had done something so special for her. He finished dishing out the stew until everyone's plates were filled.

"The china, the silver"—she gulped back the onslaught of emotion filling her—"it's all so very lovely. Really."

"I hope you don't mind I bought the china. It was as close as I could find to the ones pictured in your travel book."

"You read my book?" she asked, surprised.

"I did. I know you had your heart set on taking that big trip. I thought this might cheer you up—I mean to say, help you start to move past what happened." He stopped speaking.

Elsie's heart pounded in her chest. She realized he was trying to make amends.

He looked at her. His gaze was so intense, Elsie's breath caught in her throat.

Quietly, he said, "I thought since we'll be staying on here that it couldn't hurt to have some finer things."

She caught her lower lip between her teeth. He wanted to stay with the children. She didn't know what to make of this. Then his gaze paused on Harry and then Minnie. He nodded. They all folded their hands and bowed their heads.

Following suit, she opened her mouth to begin saying grace, but then stopped when she heard the deep timbre of Will's voice. Though she knew it wasn't polite, she lifted her head in wonder.

"Dear Lord, I know it's been a long time since you've heard from me. Even so I ask for your blessings on Harry and Minnie. I thank you for this meal set before us. Most importantly"—he stopped to clear his throat and then continued—"I want to thank you for sending Elsie to us . . . to me. Amen."

He lifted his head and looked at her. She'd heard the emotion choking his words and now saw the rich brown color of his eyes deepening with emotion. She knew this prayer had not come easily for Will. He'd been battling his faith since the day she met him, and she suspected for a long time before that. She also knew he was seeking her forgiveness. Actions did speak louder than words, and Will had just shown her in both ways that he wanted to become a better man.

Elsie said, "Thank you for saying grace." Looking at Harry and Minnie, she asked, "Shall we eat this delicious meal?"

Minnie waved her hand in the air. "Wait! Wait! I have to say grace, too." Folding her hands beneath her chin, her tiny voice filled the room.

"Lord, please don't forget I asked you to make Uncle Will and Miss Elsie happy. And thank you for this food. Amen."

Elsie dared to look at Will, who upon closer inspection did not seem at all surprised by Minnie's prayer. Frowning, she wondered if he had anything to do with this.

He shook his head, saying, "I've been meaning to tell you about Minnie's prayers."

"Let's discuss them later, shall we?"

They dug in to the stew, chattering away about the day. Every once in a while she would look up to find Will watching her. The intensity of his expression sent frissons of awareness through her. When the meal was over, the children wanted to know if they could go outside.

Elsie told them yes and then started to clear the table. Will stopped her, saying, "I'll take care of this. You go sit out on the porch and look after them."

"I want to stay inside to speak with you alone."

Together they cleared the table, and then rolling up his sleeves, Will started to fill the sink with water, preparing to wash the dishes.

Gently, she held the fine china in her hands. "I've never held anything so fragile. We'll need to store these out of the way so they don't get broken."

"Yes, we should do that." He took the first plate from her hand. His fingers lightly brushed against the tips of hers.

She couldn't stand being this close to him without touching him. Throwing caution to the wind, Elsie stood on tiptoe and kissed him on the lips. Will slid the dish into the water. His hands cupped her face as he returned her kiss with a passion she never knew existed. This kiss felt different from the others they'd shared. Her body responded differently, surprising her with the feeling that she needed more than just a shared kiss with him.

He ended the kiss first, gathering her in his strong, muscular arms. Wrapping her arms around his middle, she lay her head against his solid chest. She listened to his heart beating strong and steady. She felt their world shifting. The anger she'd been carrying around for the past week drained from her, leaving her feeling heady.

"Where do we go from here?" She wanted to know.

"Where do you want this relationship to go, Elsie?"

"I want this to work, Will. For us and the children."

"I've left the Pinkertons."

Pulling away from his hold, she gathered his face in her hands, feeling the smoothness of his skin where the barber had shaved him. He smiled against her hands. She smiled back.

"Are you happy with your decision?"

"I am."

"What are you going to do now?"

"I've taken a real job with John Oliver."

She took a minute to absorb this information. Elsie didn't know if she could just give in to what she knew he wanted from her. "If things between us change in the way you wish them to, Will, I won't be able to stay here."

"Why not?"

"It wouldn't be proper for me to live here." She hesitated, not even sure what he meant and what she wanted. "It just can't be, that's all."

"But it would be proper if I told you I loved you."

"Oh, Will. I love you, too." She laughed and kissed him again. "I still can't live here. Not yet."

"I want to make this right with you."

"I know you do. I want you to be absolutely sure the decision you made to stay here in Heartston is the right one."

"I promise you, Elsie, I made the right choice. I'll prove it to you tomorrow at the church picnic."

Chapter Twenty

Sunday dawned bright and crystal clear with pockets of mist dotting the landscape where springs and streams flowed. Will found he'd grown accustomed to the chilly Adirondack mornings marked by this light mountain fog, which would later burn off to make room for the afternoon warmth.

Today was the annual Lord's Acre Picnic. Harry and Minnie had been talking about all the games they would be playing. Harry told him last night at bedtime that he'd already picked out his teammate for the three-legged race.

Minnie informed him that she would be having a tea party under the branches of the big maple tree in the back corner of the churchyard. He felt honored that they were sharing their plans with him. However, his plans for today were of a different slant. Standing in front of the hall mirror, he worked at getting the knot on his string tie just right.

Bustling into the hallway, Elsie saw him struggling and came to him, batting his hands away. "Here, let me do this. Honestly, why men don't know how to tie their own ties is beyond me."

Crooking his mouth up into a grin, he responded with, "Maybe we just don't care enough about wearing these darn fool things to worry about learning how to put one on properly."

She let out a harrumph, finished tying the tie, and gave his chest a quick pat. "There, all done. Now where have the children gotten off to?"

"Last I saw of them, they were heading outside. I told Harry to wait for us on the porch."

She started to move by him, but Will put a hand on her arm, stopping her. He wanted a minute more to admire her beauty in peace and quiet before she became too busy to be with him. Because she was part of the committee, he knew he might not see hide nor hair of her until the end of the day. The woman had a way of becoming absorbed in whatever project she put her mind to.

"You look lovely." He told her, admiring the soft blue color of the gown she wore. He'd never seen this on her before and wondered when she'd found the time to purchase it. The cut of the dress hugged her curves. The top of the dress swooped down, exposing her fair skin. The sleeves were trimmed in delicate lace, the fabric skimming her delicate wrists.

He caught her hand in his, feeling her silky-smooth skin inside his calloused hands. He turned her hand so her palm faced up. And then he bent his head, kissing the tender underside of her wrist. Her quick intake of breath brought a satisfied smile to his lips.

"Mr. Benton!" she exclaimed.

Looking up, he could see the blush skimming her cheeks. He caught the smile she battled to hide from him. "Miss Mitchell, I hope I didn't offend you."

She shook her head. "You know you didn't. Come on, Will. I can't be late."

Bending his elbow, he placed her hand inside the crease, escorting her out the door. He retrieved the picnic basket, which contained a large pan of apple crisp. The scent of the warm apples mixing with the cinnamon and sweet brown-sugar topping set his mouth to watering, making him wish they didn't have to sit through what was sure to be an overly long outdoor sermon before the picnic.

They proceeded through the town of Heartston, looking for all the world like any other family on their way to church. And for the first time, Will felt like that was exactly what they were. A family. His family. And if he got his way, after today Elsie Mitchell would soon officially become a part of it.

The churchyard had been transformed. A huge tent had been erected in the center of a field next to the church. Outside were tables lined up in long rows. One section had been set aside and was already being filled with the food for the potluck picnic. Gaily colored streamers hung from the tree branches. Elsie took the basket with the apple crisp from him and set it on the far end of the table with the other desserts.

She'd gone as far as the oak tree when Reverend Finley's wife stopped her.

"Elsie! Elsie!" She called out her name, practically falling over her skirts as she rushed to crush her in an embrace.

Elsie disappeared in the fleshy folds of the woman's beefy arms. "My, if you aren't a sight for sore eyes! I was so distressed to learn of your run-in with that nasty excuse for a man, Virgil Jensen. Why, I knew that man was a good-for-nothing thief all along. Thank the Lord above you were unharmed."

The woman was as wound up as a top. She prattled on, telling Elsie how happy she was to see her here and how everyone had been praying for her. Then she released Elsie and set her sights on Will.

"And you! Well just look at how handsome you are. All cleaned up and dressed proper. We can't thank you enough for saving our Elsie." Mrs. Finley caught hold of his hand and shook it for all it was worth.

He smiled politely at her, catching Elsie's eye over the top of the woman's bonnet. She rolled her eyes. Will bit back a laugh.

"I have to get back to my duties. Doesn't the yard look divine? The committee did a wonderful job." Her attention shifted to another parishioner. "I have to run along now."

Elsie was now flanked by two more women. From the gist of the conversation, Will guessed they were mothers of some of her students. They were talking about what had happened and giving her hugs. By the time she managed to pry herself away from them, the church bell was ringing, signaling that the service was about to begin.

Will called to Harry and Minnie to come join them. They entered the tent, where wooden benches had been set up in two rows. In the front of the tent was a makeshift pulpit. A din of voices mingled with the sound of children's laughter. The room quieted as Will walked Elsie down the aisle to the last remaining empty seats near the front of the tent.

He felt a tingling at the base of his neck and fought the urge to itch it. Everyone was looking at them. Elsie put her hand in his, squeezing it. He squeezed back. He let Harry and Minnie enter the row ahead of them. Then, letting go of Elsie's hand, he ushered her into the seat. The pastor appeared at the front of the tent. He opened with a prayer welcoming everyone to the service.

Reverend Finley's gaze settled on them. "I'd also like to add a special blessing for William Benton. The man who saved our schoolteacher's life."

A round of applause started and ended with cheers. Will didn't quite know what to make of all this attention. His job as a Pinkerton agent had been one done in seclusion and subterfuge. No one ever knew what he did for a living. If everything went according to plan on his assignments, he'd enter a town, capture the criminal, and be on his way. No one the wiser. He wasn't entirely sure how much the townsfolk here knew of him.

He supposed it didn't matter. After today, his entire life would change. Or so he hoped.

The applause died down and the service continued. Reverend Finley read from the first Bible reading. Then he talked about forgiveness, quoting from the scriptures. Will couldn't bring himself to look at Elsie, knowing how she'd told him she wasn't ready to forgive him. He felt a hand on his and looked down to find it was hers. The service ended with the congregation singing "Amazing Grace." They stood and waited their turn to exit the tent.

Before they were even out the door, Elsie leaned into him.

"Will. Come with me for a minute."

He walked with her to the edge of the field away from prying eyes. "What's wrong?"

"Nothing. Everything. I haven't been able to stop thinking about what happened. Oh, Will. I've been such a fool. I know you were only doing your job when you came here. I never should have allowed myself to be taken in by Virgil. It was my fault. I put the children in harm's way."

"Elsie Mitchell, you listen to me. None of what happened was your fault. Believe me when I tell you how much I wanted this assignment to be over. I'm not going to tell you I regret the decisions I made. I can't say those words because finding the bond thief was my first priority."

She started to speak, and he knew if he let her do so, he wouldn't be able to say his piece. Laying a finger across her sweet, soft lips, he silenced her. "I never anticipated what it would be like to have the responsibility of being Harry and Minnie's guardian. I never knew my heart could be so full of love for them."

"Oh, Will."

"I never knew my heart could be so full of love for you, Elsie Mitchell. You came into my life like a storm. All fired up and stubborn."

"I didn't know what to make of you, either, you know. You were so secretive, and even though you tried to keep your emotions in check, I knew you were falling in love with your niece and nephew. I hoped you were falling in love with me, too." She wrapped her arms around him. "I love you, Will. I love those children. What do you say we give Minnie and Harry the family they deserve?"

Raising his eyebrows, he spoke the words he'd been rehearsing in his mind for the past two days. "I can't promise you I'll be perfect, but I can promise you that I will love you until the end of time. Elsie Mitchell, would you do me the honor of becoming my wife?"

Throwing her arms around his neck, she cried, kissing him through her tears. "Yes. Yes. Yes. I will marry you, William Benton."

Behind them, Minnie let out a squeal of delight. "I'm getting a mommy and daddy. Harry! Miss Elsie is going to marry Uncle Will. I heard her say yes!"

Picking Elsie up off her feet, he spun her around. Setting her back on her feet, he kissed her soundly. Then he picked Minnie up, her tiny arms holding tightly around his neck.

"You've made me so happy, Uncle Will." Planting a big sloppy kiss on his check, she squirmed out of his arms. "I need to tell my friends."

Will let her go. She ran through the field. Elsie stood beside him.

"There's something I've been meaning to ask you about."

"Ask me anything."

"Amy told me you donated a large sum of money to the church. Is this true?"

"Yes. I'm not sure you're going to be happy with where the money came from, though."

"No more secrets, Will, please."

"There was a reward for Virgil's capture."

"I see," she said.

"I decided to give the money to a good cause. I know how much you love your church."

She threaded her fingers through his as they started to make their way back to the picnic. "I hope you know this is your church, too."

"I do now. And one more thing, before I forget"—he pulled her to a halt—"I know you've dreamed of traveling abroad, and while we can't do it right now, I thought perhaps you wouldn't mind a honeymoon trip to New York City."

She threw her arms around him again. "Thank you."

"My pleasure if it means I'll be getting more hugs and kisses from you."

"You don't need an excuse to earn those."

It seemed Minnie had spread the word about their engagement, because by the time they reached the edge of the field, they were met by another round of cheers and applause. Pushing his way through the throng of parishioners, Harry joined them.

"I'm glad we're going to be a family."

Will ruffled his hair. "Me, too, Harry. Me, too."

While they waited their turn in the food line, Will looked on as Amy embraced a tearful Elsie. Leaning close to her, he whispered in Elsie's ear, "I love you."

"I love you, too."

They spent the afternoon enjoying good food and the company of their friends and neighbors. They stayed to help clean up. By the time the celebrations were over, the sun was dipping behind the mountain-top. Will carried a sleeping Minnie, and Elsie walked with Harry back to the house.

As they went up the front steps, he heard Elsie say, "Welcome home, Will."

Orange-and-red hues lined the skyline behind them, silhouetting his family in a soft glow. Together, Elsie and Will crossed the threshold of their house, ready to embrace a new beginning.

Acknowledgments

From the start this book has been part of a team effort. I have to thank Susan Brower, who saw my talent even when I doubted it was there. To my writing sisters, Sharon Schulze and Jo Ann Ferguson, I honestly don't know what I would do without the two of you. One word, Vegas!

To the fabulous team at Brilliance Publishing and Waterfall Press—from the editors and cover artist to marketing and author representatives—I can't say enough about how wonderfully supportive all of you are. You make the life of this author so much easier. To Jennifer Lawler, who is quite possibly the most talented developmental editor out there, thank you for bringing out the best in my writing.

And lastly, a very special thanks to Erin Calligan Mooney for adding this book to her list. I am so grateful to have you as my editor.

About the Author

Photo © 2013 Marti Corn Photography

Tracey J. Lyons is the author of many historical romance novels, including the Women of Surprise series. An Amazon Top Ten bestselling historical romance author, she is a member of Romance Writers of America, American Christian Fiction Writers, and Novelists, Inc. Her books have been translated into several languages, and she has appeared on the award-winning Cox cable television show *Page One*. Tracey lives with her family in Orange County, New York. When not busy writing, she enjoys making her husband crazy with renovation projects at their 1860s home. Visit Tracey's website at www.traceylyons.com.